WHEN THE TREES CRY

No One Can Hear Them

By
A G Nuttall

First published by A G Nuttall 2024

Copyright © 2024 by A G Nuttall

All rights reserved. No part of this publication may be reproduced, stored or transmitted in any form or by any means, electronic, mechanical, photocopying, recording, scanning, or otherwise without written permission from the publisher. It is illegal to copy this book, post it to a website, or distribute it by any other means without permission.

This novel is entirely a work of fiction. The names, characters and incidents portrayed in it are the work of the author's imagination. Any resemblance to actual persons, living or dead, events or locales is entirely coincidental.

First edition 2024

978-1-0686691-1-8 (paperback)

angiebooks.com

I would like to dedicate this book to my sister, Melanie.

CONTENTS

CHAPTER 1	1
CHAPTER 2	4
CHAPTER 3	9
CHAPTER 4	14
CHAPTER 5	26
CHAPTER 6	34
CHAPTER 7	37
CHAPTER 8	42
CHAPTER 9	47
CHAPTER 10	50

CHAPTER 11	55
CHAPTER 12	60
CHAPTER 13	65
CHAPTER 14	76
CHAPTER 15	81
CHAPTER 16	86
CHAPTER 17	93
CHAPTER 18	97
CHAPTER 19	103
CHAPTER 20	111
CHAPTER 21	116
CHAPTER 22	127
CHAPTER 23	136
CHAPTER 24	147
CHAPTER 25	153
CHAPTER 26	165
CHAPTER 27	175
CHAPTER 28	180
CHAPTER 29	185

CHAPTER 30	192
CHAPTER 31	195
CHAPTER 32	202
CHAPTER 33	207
CHAPTER 34	214
CHAPTER 35	221
CHAPTER 36	230
CHAPTER 37	236
CHAPTER 38	241
CHAPTER 39	247
CHAPTER 40	251
CHAPTER 41	260
CHAPTER 42	266
CHAPTER 43	271
CHAPTER 44	277
CHAPTER 45	287
CHAPTER 46	301
ABOUT THE AUTHOR	307

CHAPTER 1

The sound of distant humming coaxed her gently into consciousness. Surely the alarm could not be sounding already. She strained to focus on the illuminated numbers of the clock – 4:20am. The relief was overwhelming and she nestled back into the softness of her pillows knowing sleep would find her easily, but the humming continued. Reaching towards the bedside table her fingers fumbled, searching for the disturbance. She gripped the offensive object and raised it to her ear. Without opening her eyes or checking the details of its dimly lit screen she mumbled, "Hello."

"Meg, is that you?" The voice was immediately recognisable. "It's me, Della. Thank God you answered." The tone was low and the voice trembled, bearing no resemblance to the confident, harsh tones of the Della she had known in college.

Why on earth would Della Warren be calling at this hour of the night? Had she misdialled?

"Della, do you know what time it is?" whispered Meg, conscious of her sleeping partner.

Della appeared oblivious to the hour as she sobbed, "Tyla's missing."

Tyla was the youngest child of Della Warren and no more than six years old, if Meg remembered correctly.

"What do you mean by missing?"

Meg knew the Della of old was prone to theatrics and although they hadn't seen each other in quite some time, she could not imagine that Della had changed.

"She's gone, Meg, her bed's empty, she's missing, kidnapped, I just don't know what to do."

Della erupted into a flood of tears.

"Are you sure she's not just wandered downstairs, gone to the toilet, sleepwalking? Have you searched the house?" queried Meg.

"From top to bottom twice," replied the distressed Della. "I know all of her hiding places, she's not there, she's not anywhere."

"Is there evidence of a break-in?"

"No, the doors are still locked."

"And you're certain she's not in the house?"

"She's not, Meg!" Della's panicked voice replied.

"You must inform the police then," urged Meg.

"I thought you were the police?"

"Not officially, not anymore."

"Will you come, Meg? I'd feel much more comfortable with you here, I need someone I can trust beside me," begged Della.

It was easy for Meg to agree to the request. Her desire to help, to be needed, stemmed from her deep-rooted guilt for not saving her friends three years earlier. The pain she still felt at their loss could only be relieved by her desperation to save someone else. She wore the penance like a heavy weight around her neck, a symbol of failure, a constant overpowering burden.

"Okay, I'll be there in the morning. I'll take the early train."

Meg turned towards her husband and whispered, "Fin, I'm going to Wales first thing..."

Fin didn't respond even though he was awake. He felt Meg turn away and pull at the duvet. He closed his eyes though he knew he wouldn't sleep.

Finlay Castleton knew only too well the trauma of the last few years. He and Meg had experienced tragedy and loss firsthand. Their marriage had been tested to the limit and it was undeniably hanging by a volatile thread.

Meg had fought hard to imprison her demons, but therapy, religion, failed pregnancies did not relieve the burden she carried through life.

It would be futile to talk her out of visiting Wales, of that he was certain, but he worried that his wife's current state of mind would be her undoing. Of course, Meg didn't see it that way. She was the stoic Samaritan whose only purpose in life was to save those in need.

CHAPTER 2

As morning sunlight warmed platform 2 Meg emerged into the brightness, a hold-all in one hand and a coffee in the other.

She had shared a room with Della at college; not the most memorable or enjoyable experience. Della was the worst roommate ever. Her promiscuous lifestyle and unhealthy addiction to painkillers made her toxic and unpredictable.

Meg was more than happy to leave their friendship at the college doors, but for some reason Della had never forgotten the patience and kindness Meg had afforded her. She sporadically sent emails or text messages, to which Meg always responded. There was a loneliness behind Della's communications and Meg imagined that the life she portrayed in words was significantly different to the reality.

As Meg's train pulled into Aberbarry Station, the weather was inclement. She stepped down onto a rain-soaked platform and searched the handful of faces for a familiar one.

Suddenly she locked eyes with a woman whom instinct told her was Della, though her physical appearance caused Meg to doubt. As the woman walked towards her, Meg realised her instinct was right. The shock on her face must have been considerable as the rain-soaked, frail figure of Della Warren hugged her tightly.

"Meg, it's me," she exclaimed, investigating Meg's response for a hint of recognition.

"Della... you look so different," she replied, not knowing how else to describe the transformation from buxom college partygoer to the emaciated waif that stood before her.

"Well, it's been a while," scoffed Della, "not that you've changed at all."

Perhaps Meg hadn't outwardly changed, but certainly the trauma of the last few years and the tragedy that plagued her had left its scars internally.

Della led Meg to an awkwardly parked vehicle. It was so rusty it was difficult to define its original colour. Parts of it had been changed over time leaving a patchwork of mismatched tones. Della jumped into the driver's seat and leaned across to force open the passenger door. Meg peered inside as Della pushed a mound of used coffee cups and sweet wrappers to the floor. "Get in," she demanded.

Her driving was as disorganised as the contents of her car, though thankfully the journey was only short. Della pulled onto a gravel driveway and screeched to a halt, yanking at the handbrake repeatedly until the car stopped moving.

To Meg's relief, Della's home was surprisingly pleasant. An oversized, period semi spanning three floors, standing on a generous plot of land.

Inside original parquet floors dulled from years of heavy footfall crawled along the dimly lit hallway. Hand-turned spindles marched step by step to the very top of the house, wooden soldiers parading mahogany coats in vertebral splendour. Elegant fireplaces and heavy drapes, the scent of old cigars and candle wax, the aftermath of its Victorian history still evident throughout.

Outside there were obvious signs of deterioration and a desperate need for some gardening work to tackle the expanse of overgrown lawn and surrounding hedges, but it had the makings of a pleasant and comfortable family home.

For a moment Meg's mind wandered to the little cottage she shared with her husband. They had talked of extending or moving to something a little larger, hoping that their family would have expanded by now. Sadly, it wasn't to be. Three failed pregnancies indicated that children would not bless their lives. It was yet another tragedy to add to the list and Meg knew that if trying again ended the same way as before, neither she nor Fin would recover from it a fourth time.

Meg shook away her thoughts and followed Della into the kitchen.

"Nice place, Della," she began, "yours—"

"My grandparents," interrupted Della awkwardly, "they left it to me. Needs a lot of work doing and a lot of money spending on it, but it's home."

Della placed chipped China mugs on a pine dining table and ferried across a plate of biscuits and a brightly decorated teapot. "So glad you came, Meg," she said, signalling to join her at the table. "How long can you stay?"

Meg hadn't thought about the answer. She had only packed an overnight bag and caught the first train without considering the logistics. An impulsive decision in her haste to help a friend in need.

"Well let's just see where we get to, Della," suggested Meg. "One step at a time. Now tell me, did you ring the local police?"

Della nodded, though Meg was not convinced by the acknowledgement.

"You'll be better than any policeman though, Meg. You're a detective," announced Della as if that role gave her super powers that general police officers lacked.

"Della, you need all the help you can get in these circumstances," explained Meg. "You need the police for their manpower if nothing else. A search needs organising, a description of Tyla circulating and media coverage, all these things will help to find her. Has there been any news?"

Della stared into her teacup, a cascade of tears flowing down her cheeks, and shook her head.

"I think I've just been pretending it's not happening, Meg. It's just some awful nightmare that I can't wake up from, and she will come running in from the garden at any moment."

Meg placed a comforting hand on Della's; she knew only too well that feeling of despair, that longing for the moment to pass and life to resume normality, but she also knew that ignoring the situation was not the answer.

"Look, I'm here now, let's focus our emotions on bringing your little girl home."

He had gone for a walk, needing some peace and quiet, but he could still hear him, his voice constantly gnawing inside his head, slowly annihilating his sanity. He recognised the problem; it was always the same, he was hungry again, demanding and coercive. He could never satisfy his appetite. He would have to hunt, plan, catch and kill again, it was the only way to silence him.

He didn't want to do it, he made him.

Suddenly, she was there, skipping past, stopping to pick daisies from the grass where he stood. She had wandered far enough out of sight for him to make his move. The mother was chatting, engrossed in conversation, oblivious of the fate that awaited her child. This had to be the last time no matter what he said.

CHAPTER 3

"I'm going to be asking you a lot of questions, Della. Some will be intrusive, but you need to answer them as honestly as you can," warned Meg.

Della nervously wiped away the remnants of tears and began picking at the skin around her fingernails. It was a habit she performed regularly. Meg wondered if Della was still drug dependent or whether the ritual had only started since Tyla went missing.

"Okay, let's start at the beginning, tell me everything about when and how you found Tyla missing."

"I told you all that last night on the phone," sighed Della.

"I need you to tell me again, every detail you can remember even if you think it's not relevant."

"It had been a sunny day," she began. "Tyla was playing in the garden. She had one of those water pistols and was chasing Joel with it."

"Joel?" questioned Meg.

"My son, Joel. I told you when he was born, Meg, he's thirteen now."

Meg couldn't recall Della ever mentioning a son before, but then if he was a teenager, it would have been a good while ago.

"Okay, sorry, carry on."

"I called for her to come in about half an hour later, fed her, bathed her and tucked her up in bed, that's it." She shrugged.

"Let's just go back slightly. Was Joel the only other person in the garden playing with Tyla?"

"Yes, of course, there's no way in or out of the garden apart from through the house," answered Della.

"So Joel is thirteen, and Tyla?"

"Six, almost seven. It's her birthday next month." Della's eyes welled with tears but she bravely fought them back.

"There's a considerable age difference between them… Seven years. How does Joel feel about Tyla?"

"What do you mean? He's her brother, he loves her. Are you insinuating that Joel had something to do with her disappearance?"

"Della, I'm not insinuating anything, I'm merely gathering facts. In a case like this the family are always looked into first. It's a standard line of enquiry."

"So you're looking at me too?" Della shrieked.

"I'm not looking at anyone but I know how the system works, I'm merely covering all bases and preparing you for what lies ahead."

Della calmed, rubbing her arms anxiously. "Okay, I'm sorry. I understand why you're asking these questions, but it's hard, you know?"

"I do know, Della, I know better than anyone how hard a situation like this is, but you need to stay strong for Tyla and you need to do whatever it takes to give us the best chance of getting her back."

Della nodded, biting at her bottom lip.

"So you put Tyla to bed at what time?" continued Meg.

"It would be around 8pm."

"Do you have a bedtime ritual? Does Tyla sleep through the night, do you check on her at regular intervals?"

"Errr no... I kiss her goodnight, shut the door and don't usually see or hear from her until morning. She's always been a good sleeper, even as a baby."

"Okay. Now does the house have a working alarm and do you use it?"

"Well, there is an alarm but I never use it, to be honest I don't know how to. I'm not even sure that it works. Needs a code I think and I have no idea what that might be."

"You're doing great, Della, just a couple more things. Are you seeing anyone at the moment?"

Della raised her head and looked straight into Meg's eyes before answering, "What do you think, Meg? I mean look at the state of me, who's going to want a piece of this?"

Meg was taken aback by Della's destructive opinion of herself. She had always been such a confident girl, the type boys lusted after, but the Della sitting at the kitchen table bore no resemblance to that girl.

"One question I really need to ask you, Della, and I need the absolute truth." Meg waited for Della to lock eyes with hers. "Are you dependent on any kind of drugs or alcohol?"

Della's eyes brimmed once more; the question had obviously touched a nerve.

"No, Meg, not now, not anymore."

"You're clean?"

"For almost three years."

Meg wanted to ask more but the sight of Della's deflated expression stopped her.

"Can I see Tyla's bedroom, please?" asked Meg, changing the subject.

Della led her from the kitchen to the first-floor landing. From there several doors branched off; Joel's was on the left at the back of the house, Della's was in the middle and Tyla's overlooked the front garden.

As Della turned the handle and pushed the door ajar, Meg stepped inside. It was a little girl's bedroom for certain. Dolls and cuddly toys lined the window sill. The walls were dusky pink, fairy lights draped the curtains, and a collage of furry animals lined the walls. A purple pushchair played host to a one-eyed teddy bear and a mound of girls' clothing was piled high on a threadbare rug at the end of the bed. A Minnie Mouse duvet had been cast aside and the imprint of a small body left its outline where the child had laid. A dried stain on the bottom sheet indicated that Tyla had wet the bed that night.

"She doesn't usually wet the bed," impressed Della, anticipating Meg's next question.

"Strange that she did last night," commented Meg. "Anything missing?"

Della glanced around the room as if the thought hadn't crossed her mind until that moment. "I don't think so."

"No bedtime bear, favourite doll or stuffed animal?" Meg questioned, knowing how strong the bond between a child and their toy could be.

Della's eyes lit at the sudden realisation. "Yes, she has a giraffe, small, wearing a red bow tie. She usually sleeps with it, but... I don't see it anywhere."

"Della, I think it's time you make that call to the police," suggested Meg.

CHAPTER 4

It seemed no time at all before the blue light of a police vehicle flashed across the sash windows of Della's lounge.

Constables Ewan Davis and Primrose Swann from the local constabulary introduced themselves.

Ewan was around six feet tall, built like a rugby player with hair so blond it was almost white. Primrose was the complete opposite, standing no more than four feet nine and as round as she was tall. Her chubby face, red cheeks and rotund figure gave her the air of a cartoon character, save for her crop of short greying hair. Her uniform had the difficult task of keeping her fully concealed. Flashes of bare skin erupted between the buttons of her white shirt, threatening to burst forth at any moment.

Seated around Della's kitchen table with mugs of coffee the officers proceeded to ask for background information and a current photograph of the missing child.

"I take it you've checked with her father, grandparents, school, friends of the family, and so on, that she isn't with one of them?" enquired Constable Davis.

Della nodded.

"Who is her father, if you don't mind me asking?" added Constable Swann.

Della flushed instantly, a crimson glow colouring her cheeks. "Why do you want to know who her father is?" she snapped.

"It's a perfectly routine question, Miss Warren, we will need to contact him."

Della looked from one constable to the other and then towards Meg.

"Truth is I really have no idea," mumbled Della, staring down at her hands.

The constables glanced at each other, a glint of hypocrisy in their eyes.

"I see," said Constable Davis. "You have no idea at all?"

"Couldn't hazard a guess," suggested Constable Swann.

"Look, it was a one-night stand, a drunken fumble in a nightclub bathroom, that's all I remember."

Meg was listening intently. Perhaps Della Warren hadn't changed that much after all.

Constable Davis closed his notebook. "I think we have what we need for now," he stated. "We will perform a risk assessment. Tyla will be treated as a misper. I shouldn't worry too much though, little ones go missing all the time, but generally they come back when they're hungry. Trust me, I know, I have two little girls of my own."

Davis and Swann rose from the table and headed towards the door.

"Is that it then?" snarled Della, harvesting no comfort whatsoever from the constables' words. "I have to just sit here and wait to see if she comes back of her own accord. Wait for another day while God knows what could be happening to her at the hands of God knows who."

Della was visibly shaking, but the constables remained unperturbed.

"Like Ewan said, if she doesn't come back soon, we will open a missing persons case, that's all we can do for now. We will circulate her photograph between stations and ask colleagues to be on the lookout. There is nothing to suggest that Tyla has been taken against her will, no forced entry, broken windows, everything points to the child having left of her own accord," explained Primrose.

"In the middle of the night?" Della growled. "Are you serious?"

Meg knew the police officers were stalling. Tyla had been missing all night; it was highly unlikely that she had strayed out into the darkness alone. Especially as the locks on both exits were mounted higher than the reach of a seven-year-old. Budget and manpower were the sobering reasons behind their inability to rush into declaring the child anything other than temporarily 'absent'.

Meg's instincts were working overtime. Tyla Cassidy had been abducted.

Della was working herself into a stupor. If the door hadn't opened and an arrogant-looking teenager walked in there was every possibility that she would have swung for the unduly patronising Constable Swann.

"Who's this?" enquired Davis as Joel passed him on the doorstep.

"That's my son, Joel."

"Can you remember who his father is?" teased Swann.

Della made a break for the door, but Joel caught her by the arm and pulled her back, holding her tightly until the sound of the police car leaving could be heard on the loose gravel outside.

"I think they've gone," remarked Meg.

Joel loosened his grip and ascended the stairs without saying a word.

🌳

A police car passed him on the street. He waited as it disappeared from view. Coppers snooping around the area were the least of his worries.

His thoughts turned to the frightened eyes that peered at him from the cage in his basement. The flowing curls that bounced uncontrollably every time he stooped to say 'hello'. The girl had soiled herself and the smell caught the back of his throat; he retched and gagged with disgust. She had sealed her fate with such behaviour, forced him to plot her demise earlier than planned. It must be done that evening, he couldn't wait.

***

Della had taken some tablets to calm her nerves and fallen asleep on the sofa. Meg covered her gently with a patterned blanket. Her tiny body resembled that of a child's as she lay huddled beneath it.

Della had always sported a voluptuous figure. It had been her most attractive asset, a tiny waist, ample bosom and curves in all the right places. She had no difficulty in catching the eyes of randy college boys or for that matter, lecherous professors. Confident in her own skin Della had painted a portrait of sexual appeal, fun loving and vibrant.

In stark comparison, the Della who lay curled in the corner of the couch portrayed a shadow of her former self. Underweight, pallid and dejected, words Meg never imagined would be used to describe her formidable college roommate.

The house was eerily quiet; only the incessant ticking of a grandfather clock broke the silence.

Meg took the opportunity to wander into the back garden. She needed some air, some time to think.

It was almost as overgrown as the front, except for a square patch of lawn that housed a child's swing. The growth beneath it had been worn away from constant use. An abundance of wild flowers had found life around its edge, where an army of insects gathered to feast. Beyond the pleasant blooms the undergrowth grew thicker, home to a flourishing development of thistles, nettles and hazardous loose stones, the ruins of a once decorative wall.

The whole area was adequately fenced with no obvious sign of escape, though as Meg wandered further, she spied a broken fence panel positioned in such a way as to appear secure. At first sight it accomplished the job, but a keen-eyed Meg had noticed the wooden slats were slightly askew. She pulled the panel to one side revealing a good-sized hole. Poking her head through the gap she was greeted by an expanse of open meadow meandering towards a distant woodland beyond.

Meg climbed through and stood back looking towards the house, scanning the outside of its foreboding size. It was a large house for Della and two children to maintain, but she suspected they had nowhere else to live. How could Della afford the cost of utilities, let alone repairs? As far as Meg knew she hadn't worked for many years. The answer wasn't obvious. Perhaps her parents helped out financially, or Joel's dad, whoever he was.

Meg's eyes wandered upward towards the first-floor windows, where Joel was standing in the shadows watching her. He withdrew hastily at his sudden discovery; she couldn't see him but she sensed he was still there.

The house attached to Della's was appallingly neglected. Its decaying façade made Della's property appear almost pristine. Meg suspected that its owners were elderly; the giveaway grey net curtains and window boxes still bearing the remains of last year's annuals were always a telltale sign of aged occupants.

Meg sighed and dialled Fin. It was time to check in with her husband, that is if he had even noticed she was missing.

Fin answered wearily. "Bad day?" questioned Meg.

"No worse than usual," came the reply. "How about you?"

"Well I'm here in the heart of Wales with Della."

"Who's Della?"

Meg bit her lip. Della had cropped up in conversation many times during their three-year marriage, Fin was just being awkward.

"My old college roommate, the one I've mentioned in the past."

"The slutty one?"

"Yes, that one, the only roommate I had in college," growled Meg.

When Fin was in one of those moods, she should really just cut off the conversation, but she was determined not to.

"Anyway, she's very different now, she's changed a lot. I hardly recognised her at the station."

"And what exactly are you doing for her, Meg?" There was an indignation in his tone that she knew well. It occurred whenever Fin disagreed with her plans or decisions.

"Her child is missing, Fin, I'm helping find her."

"Of course you are," scoffed Fin, "can't trust the local police to do their job, can you Meg!"

A sudden combination of anger and sadness welled inside her. Tears began pooling in her eyes as she fought hard to keep them under control.

"I'll keep you updated, don't know when I'll be home. I guess a few days apart will be good for both of us."

Meg ended the call as her tears found their freedom.

***

Wiping away the aftermath of sadness, Meg discovered she had wandered unknowingly into the neighbour's garden. No fences defined its boundary, it simply flowed into the field beyond.

Meg turned to leave, aware she was trespassing, but something caught her eye. Relaxing against the grubby windowpane between a gap in the dirty curtains sat a large, black and white cat. It was preoccupied with an object that was hanging from its mouth.

As the last rays of evening sun played against the window the object winked momentarily and then the light was gone.

Meg moved closer, pushing her face against the glass. The cat was unperturbed by her presence and proceeded to paw playfully at its treasure. The object suddenly dropped from its grasp and hit the window, landing in full view on the ledge below.

Meg stared in horror at the rotting remains of a human finger. The skin had decayed, exposing a splintered area of bone around which sat a gold band, a wedding ring perhaps.

She gathered herself together. The cat had disappeared leaving its morbid prize behind. Where had it found the finger and who did it belong to?

Guiding herself against the wall of the house Meg picked her way steadily through a forest of undergrowth.

A path lay somewhere below her feet, and navigating its uneven surface made for cautious and carefully placed footsteps.

The back door to the house was unlocked. Meg hesitated. A single turn of the handle and she was inside. The stench of death and orchestra of flies gave certainty to her thoughts; she had found the source of the severed finger. She should have left the property immediately, called the police, but the detective inside her couldn't resist taking a look around.

The kitchen was alive with uninvited guests writhing and squirming across abandoned China. Cat faeces coated the floor and the smell of death grew stronger. Down the hallway Meg cautiously picked her way towards the lounge. The light had faded now, and the house was cloaked in darkness. She felt for her phone and turned it to torch mode, holding the light high in front of her as she entered the living room.

Her mind flashed back to Molecatcher Farm on that fateful evening when she had discovered the bodies of Ben and Alice Cross. Her heart was racing, jumping against her chest, beads of sweat forming across her forehead as the sight of the brutally slain couple rushed into view. Her breathing was fast and erratic. As she gasped for air, she knew death was around her, she could feel it, smell it, her mouth was dry and her hand trembled as she flashed torchlight around the room.

Suddenly she hit the ground, her hand piercing rotten flesh, her face within kissing distance of the decomposing body that had cushioned her fall. She choked, fumbling to her feet, shaking the liquified decay from her skin.

A flash of light revealed the remains of her unfortunate encounter. Laying side by side in the centre of the room were the bodies of two people. Decomposition was advanced; death had found them at least a month earlier. They had been gutted from sternum to navel, their innards displaced, ripped from their cavities and strewn across the carpeted floor. Blood had gushed, encircled their bodies and dried. The cat had feasted on their fleshiest bits in a bid to survive. Most of their finger bones had disappeared but Meg suspected they lay abandoned somewhere within the house.

The fireplace beyond sat like a headstone marking their demise. Ash spewed from its neglected grate; no fire had danced here for a long time. The framed photograph of an elderly couple stood proudly in its centre, the fated victims of a brutal crime.

It was late at night as he loaded her body into the boot of his car concealed within the confines of a black plastic bag. He shrouded the lifeless package in blankets and coats and closed the door quietly.

Releasing the handbrake, he pushed his faithful Volvo out onto the road. It was a manoeuvre he had executed many times and he performed it perfectly. As the engine purred to life he drove slowly in low gear along the avenue until reaching the junction, where he changed gear and drove swiftly towards his destination.

Aberbarry had not yet entered the digital spy era of camera coverage. The town's main street was the only place his car could be picked up on CCTV.

He was always one step ahead. Every minute detail thought through, the route travelled many times and diversions planned to avoid detection.

He checked his watch – eight minutes and fifteen seconds precisely. He parked in the shadow of an expansive oak tree and turned off the engine. He always paused for ten minutes, ensuring surprise eventualities did not catch him off guard.

As his watch alarm signalled the end of his vigil, he checked the mirrors and scanned the surrounding area for signs of life. Now to complete his mission.

He uncovered the body of the curly haired little girl and carried her towards the playground, entering from the south side, where his movements were cloaked by an army of overgrown trees.

The gate was already open; he slipped inside and headed for the centre of the play area. There he carefully positioned the child's body at the top of the smallest slide as if she were just about to take a ride down it.

He pulled a comb from his pocket and carefully ran it through the hair, arranging the curls neatly around her face. He posed her, one hand on her knee and the other holding onto the slide. He stood back to admire his work. She looked so pretty in the blue and white gingham dress he had picked out for her, the very image of a porcelain doll. Death had immortalised her. He smiled with satisfaction, turning back for a final glance before disappearing into the night.

CHAPTER 5

Meg's phone was vibrating, Della was calling.

"Where are you?" questioned a sleepy Della. "It's almost midnight. I've just woken up and you weren't here."

"I'm next door in your neighbour's house."

"At the Pipers'? Whatever are you doing there? I thought they were away visiting family."

"Well if these two bodies belong to the Pipers, they've definitely gone away but not to visit family," Meg responded.

A moment later Della came racing to Meg's side.

"Stop right there, Della, you don't need to see this," begged Meg.

Della hovered in the doorway of her neighbour's lounge, the cover of darkness shrouding her from the horrors that lay inside.

"What's that god-awful smell?" She retched, covering her mouth.

"I'm afraid it's the Pipers."

The noise outside had woken him. Blue lights flashing, people talking, quite a commotion had erupted. He hoped they hadn't woken him too. He was difficult to handle at the best of times, interrupted sleep would make him even more unbearable.

He poked his nose around the curtain. Something was happening at the Pipers' house. A break-in most likely. Thankfully they weren't at home, he had been feeding their cat.

***

Celia Tucker, two doors down from the Pipers but on the opposite side, knew exactly what was going on. She saw everything from her seat by the window. Confined to her home in the aftermath of a disabling stroke, the comings and goings of her neighbours was her newfound and only hobby.

Devoid of speech save for the odd uncoordinated groan, Celia found communication difficult. An untimely blood clot had stolen it from her along with the use of her right side, and partial paralysis of her left. She'd been lucky, they said at the hospital. Had she? She would have considered death a luckier option.

Celia had no family, though she was visited daily by her carer Marjorie and the on-call district nurse. The nurse had urged her to stay in bed, but what could she see from there? The faded roses on the bedroom wallpaper, the mini-TV they had placed at the foot of the divan and the comings and goings of the only two people who stopped Celia dying from social boredom.

She had opted for a comfortable chair by the bedroom window, and the mini-TV facing her from the night stand. A small table housed her TV remote, a sippy cup and a red button that she could press if ever she were in distress. Celia had just enough movement in her left arm to press buttons and lift her cup unless it was more than half full.

Celia had noticed a man visiting the Pipers' house on several occasions. Marjorie had told her the couple were away visiting family, but Celia knew the Pipers had no family.

She had been watching and mentally documenting the movements of her neighbours for the last five years, at least the ones that were visible from her window. She knew everything about them, but they knew nothing about her.

***

Meg and Della returned home just as the first light of a new day hailed its presence. There was nothing either of them could do now; the local police had arrived and the Pipers' house was officially a crime scene. They had ferried hot tea and biscuits to the busy officers working through the night, but Meg was feeling weary. Sleep deprivation clawed at her body and her eyelids fought desperately beneath the heavy weight of tiredness.

In the attic bedroom of Della's Victorian house she crawled beneath the duvet and allowed sleep to devour her.

***

She awoke hours later to a message from Fin –

'sorry about yesterday, stay safe ♥'

She hadn't had time to update him on her latest find, or rather she'd chosen not to. So much had happened in the twenty-four hours since her arrival and usually she would have been desperate to share it, but their relationship had been spiralling out of control, heading for disaster, and the distance between them made sharing seem pointless.

She dialled Fin's number, then cancelled it. She was just about to tap out a message on the blank screen when a piercing scream had her racing from the bedroom and hurdling down the stairs.

In the kitchen Della was standing in front of the TV, her mouth agape as the last muted scream found its escape. She was holding the remote in one hand and tugging violently at her long, wavy hair with the other. A sheer look of terror framed her face as she stared at the screen.

Meg grabbed the remote and adjusted the volume. 'Breaking news' flashed the headline: "CHILD POSE KILLER STRIKES AGAIN."

Della was crying now. "My baby, my baby."

Joel appeared unaware of his mother's distress. He placed headphones around his neck and rushed to Della's side, pulling her towards him and folding his arms around her. He glanced towards Meg, his face questioning, searching for the answer to his mother's emotional state.

Meg didn't know what to say. She had never heard of the child pose killer, nor did she have any details to confirm that the unfortunate child in question was Tyla Cassidy, but Joel needed comfort too.

"A child's been found, a girl… We don't know if it's Tyla," began Meg, but before she could say any more Joel raced from the kitchen and disappeared.

"Joel!"

Joel was gone, the hard slam of the front door said so.

Meg turned to Della who was sobbing into her hands.

"Let's not jump to conclusions, Della, it probably isn't her," she soothed, but Della found no comfort in the words. She grabbed a coat from the hallway and headed towards the door.

"Where are you going?" Meg called after her.

"I'm going to find out." And with that Della was heading down the gravel driveway in her pyjamas and slippers.

Meg didn't hesitate; she rushed after her, almost jogging to keep pace with Della's quick steps.

At the end of the road they turned a sharp right, crossed to the other side and followed the path down an alleyway and into an open field. Della's steps quickened as she caught sight of the police patrol ahead of her and the children's play area just beyond.

Marching with all the might of a bulldozer Della crashed through the cordoned barrier and headed towards the crime scene. A startled constable grabbed her just before she entered the white tented area that housed the victim's body.

"You can't go in there. What do you think you're playing at?" he bawled.

"I'm sorry, Officer, my friend thinks the victim could be her missing little girl," explained Meg.

The constable's face softened, but he maintained his grip on Della, pulling her further away from the white tent.

"You don't want to go in there, miss, let's get you in a car until we have something to tell you."

"Thank you." Meg praised the young officer's ability to interpret the situation and his empathy towards Della. He reminded her of Will Thackeray; he would have reacted in just the same way.

As an unmarked car drove towards the edge of the park, Meg recognised its occupant, DCI Rory McGurn. Rory had been an inspector when Meg joined the Met. She had worked alongside him on several occasions. He was a hard taskmaster but a sound policeman with forty-plus years of experience under his belt.

McGurn exited the car and lit his signature pipe. His eyes met Meg's and he acknowledged her with a nod of his head.

McGurn made his way towards the taped cordon and ducked beneath it. "My god, Quinn, what the hell are you doing in my neck of the woods? Don't tell me the Met have sent you?"

He was obviously not up to date with Meg's life story, nor her change of name, but she was thrilled that her old governor had remembered her.

"No, sir, those days are long gone. Besides…" Meg glanced down at her Snoopy pyjamas and white pumps. McGurn laughed, realising Meg's attire was not standard issue for an officer of the law.

"Quite," he sniggered without removing the old pipe from his lips. "Bad do this, though, second child in as many months."

Meg was shocked. She hadn't heard of 'the child pose killer.' Brightmarsh was not a leading source of breaking news, but the details of a child murder usually reached its sleepy existence.

"Really, sir? That's shocking! Any leads?"

"Nothing to speak of. Anyhow, I best get this over with."

McGurn sauntered in the direction of the white tent and disappeared from view.

A few minutes later he emerged, patting the back of a pale-faced young officer. *First murder,* thought Meg. *Always challenging.*

As the young PC hastily sought privacy to expel the contents of his stomach McGurn headed towards his car.

Meg followed, desperate for answers.

"Sir... Sorry, sir," she spluttered as McGurn turned to face her. "Any idea who the child is?"

McGurn said nothing, but his expression sought an explanation.

"It's my friend." Meg pointed towards the weary-looking Della sitting in the back of a parked police car. "Her girl's missing, she just needs to know if it's her."

McGurn had aged, years spent in the serious crimes unit having taken their toll. The lines on his brow resembled sheet music and furrowed as he squinted, like the ridges of a newly ploughed field. A pattern of wrinkles had mapped a course across his face as he puffed enthusiastically at his pipe. His eyes had dulled, the sparkle they once knew tarnished by the gruelling scenes they had experienced.

He cast a glance towards Della, his eyes mellowing at the sight of yet another possible grieving mother. "Okay, bring her to the station this afternoon, she can identify the child."

"Thank you, sir, I will." Meg turned to leave, but McGurn called after her.

"Better come with her, Quinn," he suggested, knowing that Della might need the support.

CHAPTER 6

He'd done it again, hit the headlines. He would be furious at the media attention he had stirred up. What was he to do? If he didn't like it then he should do his own dirty work, but oh no, he wouldn't get his hands dirty, not a chance.

His penchant for little girls was taking over their lives. It was getting risky, too, moving was becoming a chore and neither of them was getting any younger. His luck was sure to run out and who would get the blame? Who would end their life in prison? Not him, that's for sure.

He turned his attention back to cleaning the cage, scrubbing and bleaching until the stench of the recent child was gone. He burnt the clothes just like he told him and boiled the knives.

He didn't like children and he knew that, but he always looked after them. He washed and dressed them, styled their hair, picked out the appropriate places where they would be found, and they always were.

He didn't leave them in shallow graves for creatures to feast on, he didn't dismember their bodies or torture them either, he was too kind for that. He was the one with the temper, the one who had lost control on occasion, leaving a mess to clean up. He didn't care what became of them afterwards.

The cleaning was finished at last.

He counted the wooden steps that exited the basement, and stopped at seven, his lucky number. He lifted the loose carpet and folded it back. The backboard wasn't fitted like the rest; he had given it a hinge and a magnetic clasp. He pressed against it and it fell forward revealing a concealed space behind from where he lifted an old, dinted biscuit tin. It still bore traces of the colourful Christmas scene it had once so vibrantly displayed. Of course it was faded now, hidden from view for so many years, but it housed his greatest treasures.

He checked over his shoulder and listened for a moment. It was quiet, he was alone.

Carefully he lifted the tin and placed it on his knee. His heart was thumping with excitement, his fingers trembling as he lifted the lid. His face beamed as he peered inside. One by one he removed the treasures from their home and laid them on the step above. His eyes were dancing from one to the other; he felt like a child. Which was his favourite? Did he even have a favourite? It was hard to pick between them, but if he had to choose one… He lifted high a plaited lock of hair, blonde hair with a diamanté bobble attached. He held it close and breathed in deeply, holding his breath as the faintest whiff of scent tickled his nostrils. He brushed it against his cheek, enjoying its silky caress upon his skin. It was so soft, so beautiful, so special, it was his first.

A noise upstairs interrupted his euphoria and in an instant the treasures were gone, entombed once more inside the wood step.

"It's only me," called the voice.

CHAPTER 7

Aberbarry Police Station had found its home in a disused bank. From the outside it still gave the same appearance, but inside was modern and spacious, filled with a plethora of desks and technical equipment. There was a vibrant atmosphere, voices buzzing, phones ringing and the clicking of busy keyboards. For a moment Meg was back in the past, a young constable herself fresh from college and eager to save the world.

"This way, ladies." Meg was back in the moment and following the voice down a corridor to a nearby waiting area.

"There's tea or coffee while you wait," suggested the voice, signalling to an automatic drinks machine at the end of a row of empty chairs.

Della was pale and trembling.

"I could do with more than a coffee," she'd said to Meg as the police officer turned away.

"It will be over soon," soothed Meg. "Are you sure you want to do this? I can go on my own, I know what Tyla looks like."

Della shook her head defiantly. "No. She's my daughter, Meg, I should be the one to do it."

"It probably isn't her, Della. Let me check first, please."

But Della was adamant that she would carry out the identification herself. Meg had tried to explain the process, warned her that the experience could be horrifying, even life changing. Once seen it was never to be unseen. The stuff of nightmares. Meg had witnessed death, lived with the trauma of mutilated bodies, and knew the damage it inflicted. She had no idea what Della was about to face, McGurn had not revealed details of the child's fate, but whatever, the sight of a dead body was traumatic, let alone that of a small child who could also be your daughter.

A door opened and McGurn himself was standing there.

"Ready?" he asked, a solemn look upon his face.

Della rose from her seat and followed. He paused in the corridor and placed a hand on her shoulder. "You certain you want to do this, Ms Warren?"

Della nodded.

Meg knew that once Della disappeared inside that room there was no going back. Whatever horror she was about to face, whether it was her child or not, it would live with her for the rest of her life.

At the last moment Della turned and reached out a hand towards Meg, who grasped it firmly and walked beside her into the dimly lit room.

McGurn ushered them towards the glass screen, then nodded to the waiting mortician on the other side.

The man took hold of the white sheet that was covering the small body and pulled it gently aside.

Della let out a loud gasp, an impulsive reaction as the child lying in front of her was not Tyla.

She left the room immediately, overcome by emotion. The child wasn't hers but she cried for the poor mother whose child it was.

Meg stood silent, gazing upon the little girl's face. She was pale and still, she could have been mistaken for sleeping, but the waxy complexion, the statuesque posture and the absence of breath told her otherwise.

McGurn signalled the mortician to unveil the child's body, revealing ligature marks around the hands and ankles, the signs of restraint, bruising around her neck and most disturbing of all, the knife wound that sliced through her tiny torso from sternum to pelvis.

"My god, poor thing," uttered Meg. "Strangulation and stabbing?"

"Strangulation, no. The pathologist thinks it was something she wore that caused the bruising, a type of collar possibly. Ever seen anything like this before?" queried McGurn.

"Yes," replied Meg, turning to face him, "though not on a child. I discovered two bodies yesterday in the house next door to Della's. An elderly couple had been slain and slashed in exactly the same manner."

"Good god," replied the DCI, startled. "You think they could be related?"

"Possibly. Forensics on the type of knife should tell you more, but in my experience it's extremely unlikely for the same killer to target adults and children, usually there's a definitive preference."

"Mine too, Quinn. I can only hope this is a coincidence," stated McGurn.

"When children are involved it's usually the result of paedophilia," added Meg.

"There's no sign of sexual abuse, but we're dealing with one sick bastard, that's for sure. I think it's safe to say we're looking for a serial killer."

"Any trace of DNA?"

"Nothing at all. The killer is fastidious, well-practised, intelligent. We have absolutely nothing to go on, except two dead children."

Meg knew the despair and frustration of working a case with no leads; the sudden high of a possible connection and the instant nosedive into depression when the lead goes cold. "How is it that I haven't heard of the 'child pose killer?'" she questioned.

"We tried to keep it away from the media as much as possible, played it down for the sake of the public. Aberbarry isn't used to morbid publicity, this sort of thing never happens here. Then some smart-arsed young journalist from the *Herald* got a hold of it. He's written a no-holds-barred piece on the front page and headlined it 'the child pose killer'. You can imagine the backlash."

"Sounds to me like you have a mole in your midst," declared Meg. She was intrigued.

CHAPTER 8

When Della was settled safely at home and Joel was back in his room, Meg borrowed the rusty old jalopy of a car and headed into Aberbarry.

It was late afternoon as she pulled into the car park at the back of the newspaper building and climbed the steps to its elaborate reception. A fusty-looking, middle-aged woman in tight blue blazer and oversized spectacles sat behind a modern, black granite desk.

"Can I help you?" she asked officiously. There was a sting in her voice that was almost as sharp as the point of her nose.

"I'd like to see Mr Rockwell, please?"

"Would that be Senior or Junior?"

Meg hadn't realised there were two Mr Rockwells, but she opted for the Junior, remembering that McGurn's description had labelled him as 'young'.

"Do you have an appointment?"

"I'm afraid not, but I'm sure Mr Rockwell would be interested in talking to me."

The receptionist's waspish smirk told Meg that Mr Rockwell Junior couldn't be seen without an appointment.

"Friday at three is the next free slot in his diary."

"Yes, that's fine," acknowledged Meg, pretending to make a note on her mobile, but of course, she wasn't going to wait almost a week.

"Thank you for your help Ms... Farley. Err could you point me in the direction of the ladies' room, please? Time of the month you know, horrendous."

Ms Farley appeared flustered at Meg's intimate confession. Her face flushed a bright shade of crimson and she spluttered as she directed Meg towards the restrooms.

Meg couldn't help but smile to herself; it worked every time, even more so with men.

Just around the corner she passed the ladies' toilet and found the lift area. Mr Rockwell Junior's name was listed on a glass plaque, he resided on the sixth floor.

Meg stepped out onto highly polished concrete and a spacious waiting area, hosting three huge, green, velvet sofas. There was an empty glass reception desk decorated with fresh pink roses and the obligatory 'Reception' sign.

To both sides, the offices were separated by glass walls, some clear, some opaque. These were very plush surroundings for such a lesser-known paper as the *Herald*.

Most of the rooms looked empty except for one. Shadowed against the opaque wall was the outline of two people. Meg knew instantly the reason the reception desk was empty. As she neared the room, she could hear voices and giggling. Mr Rockwell Junior and the missing receptionist were intimately engaged on the other side of the glass. A single tap on the door stopped them in their tracks, as the giggles turned to panic and a rather feeble, "Just a minute, please."

Seconds later, a young woman emerged, straightening her skirt as she hurried past Meg without so much as a glance. The door was ajar, Meg stepped inside.

A scarlet-faced man in his thirties was perfecting his hair. He stiffened, realising Meg was watching him.

"I'm sorry, do we have an appointment?" he asked abruptly, obviously embarrassed by his 'caught in the act' moment.

"No, but I'm here now and you don't seem to be that busy," mused Meg.

The man smiled. "Touché!" He strode towards his desk and sat down. "What can I do for you?" he asked, brushing a hand through his mop of dark curls.

"I'd like to talk to you about the child pose killer."

She'd got his attention. "Really? What do you want to know?" He waited, playing nervously with the papers on his desk.

"I want to know what you know, Mr Rockwell, and why you thought it wise to write about a child killer just to increase the sales of your newspaper."

Rockwell looked confused. "I'm sorry, who are you?" he demanded.

"I'm a police officer," lied Meg. "Your greed could just have jeopardised our whole police operation."

"Now wait just a minute," scolded Rockwell. "I was given the story by one of your own."

Just as she had suspected, Aberbarry Police Station housed a mole, but why would a police officer release information to a journalist?"

"Can I have the name of the source, please?"

Rockwell paused. "I can't reveal my source, it's confidential."

"Okay, Elliot Rockwell, I'm arresting you for withholding evidence." It was a risky move, but it just might work, hoped Meg. "You have the right to remain silent. Anything—"

"Stop!" cried Rockwell. "It's Alex, Alex McGurn."

Meg felt the air leave her body as though someone had just punched it out of her. She couldn't believe that DCI McGurn's son, Alex, was the mole. Alex had joined the force just as Meg was leaving. He was a cocky young man, but showed a lot of promise and she knew her old boss was proud of his career choice.

"Oh my god, what do I do now?" Meg was thinking out loud.

"You know him?" queried Rockwell.

"Yes, I know him, his father too, this will tear him apart."

"Fancy a drink?" proffered Rockwell, lifting a bottle of brandy in the air. "You look like you need one."

Meg sat down. "Why not?"

An hour later Meg found herself enjoying Elliot Rockwell's company. The entitled young man sported an impressive law degree, a dry sense of humour and extensive amounts of charm. Most of all he made her laugh, something she hadn't done in a very long time.

Elliot had worked his way through the company from the post room to his current position, earning his place through dedication and hard work and at the same time gaining the respect of his fellow colleagues.

The evening closed as Meg drove away in Della's jalopy with Elliot's phone number sitting in her coat pocket.

CHAPTER 9

The following morning Constable Swann arrived at Della's home, this time in her capacity as Family Liaison Officer.

Tyla had not returned home and the discovery of the little girl's body in the playground had prompted the local police to take her disappearance seriously. Searches began of secluded areas and divers took to bodies of water in and around Aberbarry. DCI McGurn was assigned to the case.

"Quite the workload I've accrued since you came into town," he had joked with Meg.

McGurn was currently investigating the child murders, and the disappearance of Tyla Cassidy. If the Pipers' post mortem revealed signs of foul play, he would most likely inherit that case too.

***

It was early afternoon when McGurn wandered into the kitchen of Della's home and took a seat beside her. He placed a stubby-fingered hand on her shoulder and patted.

"Tyla was not lying on that mortuary slab yesterday, nor will she be as long as I have anything to do with it. I'm going to do everything within my power to bring your little girl home," he soothed.

Della turned to face him and smiled.

"I do need to speak to your son, though, is he here?" McGurn's tone had sharpened and Meg knew its inference. McGurn suspected Joel of somehow being involved.

Della was nonplussed. "Why do you need to speak to him? He's got nothing to do with Tyla's disappearance."

"I just need to ask him a few questions, that's all."

"He'll be home from school soon," replied Della, taking note of the time on the wall clock.

McGurn hesitated for a moment. "What do you know about Reuben Cassidy, and is he Tyla's father?"

The question stirred Della into a whirlwind of emotions. Her eyes widened and she stuttered as she searched for a reply. "Why are you asking about Reuben?" She rose from the table and paced the length of the kitchen. "Has Reuben got something to do with Tyla's disappearance?" Della's pace quickened. She was clearly agitated by the thought of Reuben Cassidy, whoever he was.

"It's merely a line of enquiry, Della, it's been brought to my attention that Reuben is your son's father. I need to rule him out, that's all," replied McGurn calmly.

Della bit at her fingers in desperation. "I'll kill him if he's involved," she growled.

"I think there's been enough killing in this town without you adding another one to the list."

McGurn's phone sang from inside his pocket and he rose to answer it. His face was stern as he listened intently to the voice at the other end.

"Okay, thanks." The conversation ended as McGurn directed his gaze towards Meg. "Just what I needed."

Meg looked puzzled. "Bad news, sir?"

"The bodies in the house next door are now a murder enquiry."

McGurn leaned across the table towards Meg and lowered his tone. Della was being comforted by Constable Swann and both were out of earshot by the back door.

"The pathologist has identified the same knife used on the Pipers as that also used to kill the little girl."

Meg took a moment to digest the information. Did this mean that the couple were victims of the child pose killer, and if so, why? Did they perhaps know his identity?

"What does this mean, sir? Are you looking at the same person for the child killings and the couple next door?"

"It appears that we are, Quinn," came his reply.

CHAPTER 10

In the neighbouring town of Llangoffey lived a community of travellers, including the infamous Cassidys. The family were engaged in all manner of illegal activity, all of which frustrated the local police who were powerless to prosecute without hard evidence. The Cassidy clan were experts at not getting caught and each generation that emerged seemed to get more cunning and clever than the last.

Everyone knew that crimes committed in and around the area were mostly the responsibility of the Cassidys but no one could prove it, leaving the family revelling in a sense of immunity.

Over the years the small family that had initially parked their mobile homes in Llangoffey had grown immensely, now resembling a permanent holiday park for travellers. At the very heart of the community was Gerald Cassidy.

A short, muscular man whose interests included women and drink. He had fathered half the children in the area and kept order using the back of his hand and the clench of his fist.

Rhoda, his wife of thirty-plus years, paid his dalliances no attention as long as he showered her with enough money to keep her happy. She had borne him eight children, the eldest being Reuben, now aged twenty-six. At forty-two, babies were no longer an option; her body had finally called time on reproduction. Her ninth was stillborn and she was advised that any more would be too risky.

Rhoda had played her part, kept house and never asked questions. Now was her time to reap the reward of years of hard work tending to her family's needs.

Reuben was a chip off the old block. His father was his hero and he did everything he could to make Gerald proud. He'd met Della at the local club; she was older than him but Reuben didn't care. A couple of dates later Della moved in sporting the shape of a three-month pregnancy.

Joel Cassidy made his appearance on a converted sofa in Miri's van, Reuben's eldest sister who had five children of her own by age twenty-two and was adequately adept at home births.

Della hated life at the camp site, a prisoner to motherhood and an imposter in the Romany community, but her son was a Cassidy and they never turned away one of their own. Della knew she could run if she wanted but Joel would have to stay behind, so she tolerated life there for the sake of her child.

Then the opportunity came for her to make her break, when the camp was raided and Reuben was arrested and served a short sentence in prison. In the madness of the evening Della saw her chance and took it. She disappeared to her grandparents' home in Aberbarry, a place Reuben and his family knew nothing about.

It took almost a year for the Cassidys to discover her whereabouts by which time Joel had started primary school. Of course Reuben, enraged by Della's betrayal was determined to make life as uncomfortable as possible. Even a restraining order wasn't going to stop him seeing his son and he threatened Della that unless she agreed to his terms, she would never see Joel again.

Joel spent his early years ferried between parents, a situation that was far from ideal and Della lived in constant fear that each time she placed her child in Reuben's care would be the last.

As the flush of manhood began to emerge in Joel, Della had new concerns. If Joel chose to live with his father now, she would have to respect that decision, but her biggest fear was that the impressionable teen would become embroiled in the Cassidy family business of corruption. She could already recognise the signature swagger and air of indifference that the Cassidys carried about themselves slowly developing in him. She could not bear for him to become a duplicate of his father, but right now with her daughter missing Della had more to worry about.

Joel, enticed by the lack of rules and restrictions, embraced the Cassidys wholeheartedly.

In his early years spending time in the community was unnerving, a world apart from the solitary existence he spent with his mother and great grandparents.

Great-Grandpa Warren was a stickler for regulations. "You eat that or go hungry; children should be seen and not heard; elbows off the table; always remember your manners; bedtime is non-negotiable," to list but a few.

The stark difference he found at the Cassidys' was refreshing and Joel grew to love his days spent with his father and Papa Gerald.

He regularly visited after school and on the weekend. His many cousins, especially Kezia, a distant second cousin, were always happy to see him and Joel soaked up their attention, something he rarely experienced from his mother.

Kezia made his pulse race and his heart leap in his chest. Her dark curls and hazel eyes stirred feelings he hadn't experienced before. Joel was in love.

Reuben was eager to indoctrinate his young son into the Cassidy lifestyle. He allowed him to drink and try cigarettes, even offering him a joint of weed on his twelfth birthday. He taught him how to break into and hot wire a car. How to shoot a rifle and why education was a waste of time.

At first, Joel was overawed by the freedom the Cassidys afforded him, but he was soon to learn that even freedom came at a price. Papa Gerald was a scary character, even more so after a few cans of lager, when his voice grew louder and his actions wilder. Joel, however, found himself wanting to please the fearsome patriarch and receive his blessing, allowing himself to become embroiled in the seedier side of the Cassidy business. Once he had taken that first step there was no going back, even though regret was feeding on his conscience.

He did it for Kezia, who he hoped would become his future wife. He wanted to show her that he had the guts to do what it takes to look after a family. As soon as he reached sixteen, he would ask for her hand and they would be given their own property on the family estate as a result. Romas marry at a young age. Baba Rhoda was only sixteen when she wed Gerald and gave birth to Reuben in that same year.

However, Joel had also grown up under the watchful eye of Great-Grandpa Warren and his moral code, and found himself torn between a great divide. On the one hand, Reuben and Gerald Cassidy led him down a lawless road, and on the other, Great-Grandpa Warren's discipline guided him back to the right path.

The façade Joel displayed in the company of the Cassidys did not reflect his true personality. He discovered that he was not cut out for the Romany lifestyle even if it meant leaving Kezia behind. For the time being he would continue portraying his alter ego, secretly hoping that one day the gypsy kings would lose their crowns.

CHAPTER 11

The search for Tyla Cassidy was at a standstill. DCI McGurn was juggling the Piper murders, the child pose killer and the hunt for Della's daughter. The usual quota of officers was at maximum capacity, split between the three crimes currently haunting Aberbarry.

Evidence indicated that the same knife had been used to commit the Piper murders and that of the children. This discovery confirmed to McGurn that their murderer and the child pose killer were one and the same person, but the lack of DNA or significant leads made identifying him impossible.

***

When Joel Cassidy returned from school the detective was waiting.

"Sit down, young fella, just need to ask you a few questions."

Joel slowly took a seat, eyeing the policeman with suspicion.

"No need to worry, Joel," added Della in an attempt to soothe the situation, "the inspector just wants to ask you about Tyla."

Joel shifted uneasily in his seat, his cheeks a glowing shade of magenta.

"What can you tell me about the night of your sister's disappearance?" he began.

Joel thought for a moment before answering. "Can't really tell you anything. Went to bed that night and when I got up in the morning Mum said she was gone."

"What time did you go to bed, can you remember?"

"Bout 10 maybe, dunno. Did some homework, listened to music and fell asleep."

Della smiled lovingly as Joel explained.

"You didn't see or hear Tyla at any point during the night?"

"No!" confirmed Joel.

McGurn sighed heavily, glancing at Meg and then back to Joel. "You never came out of your room that night?"

"No," Joel persisted.

"Not even to raid the fridge, grab a drink or perhaps unlock the back door and let someone in?"

Joel was purple now, his cheeks puffed outwards ready to explode.

"What the fuck!" Joel snapped, grabbing his school bag and racing towards the back door.

"Joel, where are you going?" Della pleaded, but Joel gave no explanation as he slammed the door and disappeared.

"Well thanks very much," hissed Della turning to McGurn. "Not only am I missing a daughter, but now I could be missing a son."

"He'll be back soon enough," dismissed McGurn.

"I hope you're right or you'll be looking for two missing children."

Della left the room in a frenzy of muttered expletives. McGurn seemed unperturbed.

"You really think Joel had something to do with this?" queried Meg.

"It's a possibility. There's nothing to suggest someone broke into the house, but the child is missing. Locked doors and closed windows suggest to me that it was an inside job. I'm pretty certain it wasn't the mother, that leaves one other person, Joel," explained the detective.

Meg understood his reasoning. In a case like this it was sometimes just a simple process of elimination.

"And you think Joel's father might be involved too?"

"Well now that's the other reason I suspect the boy." He paused, tapping the base of his pipe on the table. "When I found out Reuben Cassidy was the boy's father alarm bells started ringing. Reuben is never one to pass up an opportunity and I think that's exactly what this is. I just need to work out how snatching the child could benefit a man like that and that's what troubles me."

"How so?" queried Meg.

McGurn inhaled deeply, the contents of his pipe flickering to life. "Trafficking or exploitation."

Meg's heart sank. The thought of sweet little Tyla in the hands of strangers with unimaginable motives was nauseating.

"Oh my god... Could this Reuben guy actually be mixed up in something like that?" Meg was horrified.

"Anything that involves hard cash, I'm afraid, and little girls can fetch a pretty penny these days. Sickening as it is, it's the reality of today's society."

McGurn rose from the table. "If you're around for a while I could use your expertise."

Meg nodded. "I'll let you know."

***

Fin was still at work and didn't appreciate being interrupted, but Meg needed him to know that she had decided to stay on at Della's until the case was solved.

"So that's it, is it?" he scolded. "No discussion, you've decided."

"Pretty much, my old inspector needs some help so I'm staying. Besides, Della needs the company and be honest, Fin, have you really noticed I'm not there?"

The line went quiet, then Fin's voice, softer in tone, uttered, "Of course I have, Meg, I miss you."

His words were sincere but Meg had decided that she was staying and no amount of flattery was going to change her mind.

"I'll stay in touch. Hopefully it won't be for too long." She heard the words leave her mouth but the reality was that she didn't believe any of them. The loneliness of living with another person had become overwhelming. It was nobody's fault. Perhaps they had rushed into marriage before the wounds of the past had healed, looking for something to ease the pain.

"I hope you find what you're looking for, Meg, I really do."

CHAPTER 12

As the light of a new day dawned, Meg skimped on breakfast and hurried off in the direction of Aberbarry Police Station.

McGurn had already arrived; he was busying himself in the briefing room waiting for his team to congregate.

"Thought I'd take you up on that offer, sir," she declared.

McGurn turned, a huge smile crossing his lips. "Excellent, excellent, come on in."

The evidence board had been split into three sections, one for each of the ongoing investigations. Tyla's sweet little face sat at the top of the first. Beneath her photograph were the images of Joel and Reuben Cassidy. Meg studied them closely. Joel was a younger, slimmer version of Reuben, both dark haired and hazel eyes, with a strong jawline, it was easy to see the family resemblance.

The second section held the grisly images of Mr and Mrs Piper.

The third was the most harrowing, as the gruesome snaps of two murdered little girls were pinned side by side across the board.

As the team gathered, DS Tully handed out briefs and Meg stood to one side as McGurn took to the floor.

"Right then. Settle down, everyone. Let's get to it. Firstly, the missing girl, Tyla Cassidy. No evidence to suggest a break-in or forced entry. Nothing missing except for a cuddly giraffe but the fact is, child was plucked from her bed in the middle of the night and disappeared. My money's on this guy." He stabbed a finger on the face of Reuben Cassidy.

The team erupted and muttering rumbled around the room.

"Yes, okay, I know how we all feel about the Cassidys, but as we also know, we need hard evidence before we can bring one of their lot in for questioning. I suggest we pay the travellers at Llangoffey a visit. Tully, Briggs, you're on that."

The two officers acknowledged the request with a toss of the head and a knowing glance.

"What's the latest from child protection?" asked McGurn, throwing the question to DS Tully.

"Nothing to report yet, sir. They're still trawling through images looking for the girl. Briggs has compiled a list of local paedos and we're eliminating one at a time, but it's slow work."

"Okay, stick with it. I want to know immediately if we get a hit," demanded McGurn.

McGurn moved across the board and studied the remains of the Pipers.

"This couple, Eva and Edward Piper, both in their eighties. Decomposition puts their deaths at approximately a month ago. Similar MO to the children, same type of knife and that's where the similarity stops for now. The neighbour, Della Warren, also the mother of our missing child, said she thought they were away visiting family or on holiday."

"So are you saying the same person committed both crimes?" mused PC Swann.

"Did you hear me say that, Constable?" McGurn grimaced.

"Not exactly, sir, no, but..."

"There are no buts in my cases, Constable, only facts. There is a similarity and that's all we have at the moment, okay?"

"Yes, sir. Sorry, sir," apologised the embarrassed officer.

"We need to go door to door in that area. As far as we can ascertain the Pipers have no family. Their passports were found in the house. It's possible they were holidaying in England as their car is not on the drive. Someone must know something about them. What was the motive here? Judging by the state of the house they were not rich people and the fact there was no break-in suggests to me this was not a robbery gone wrong. The Pipers knew their killer and allowed him or her into their home.

"Swann and Davis, you take this. Find out everything you can about the Pipers from their neighbours, get me a timeline of their last movements and speak to everyone in the vicinity."

The two constables smiled in tandem. There was nothing they loved more than a good old chin wag and a cup of tea.

"Finally…" McGurn stood for a moment as he surveyed the faces of the slaughtered children; his emotion was palpable. The whole room was eerily silent as they waited for him to speak.

"Patrick Grayson, our new DI, will fill you in on this one," he announced.

Patrick edged his way to the front of the room to the roar of jeers and claps. He'd made DI after years of working as a DS with the Aberbarry serious crimes division. He was obviously popular and as he took his place beside McGurn, it was easy for Meg to see why. Patrick wore a rugged demeanour with an athletic build, his smile lit the room and his eyes were the colour of sapphires. Constable Swann was practically salivating at the sight of him, in fact most of the female officers were.

"Thanks, everyone," he began. "It appears we have a serial killer in Aberbarry and a pretty brutal one at that. We tried to keep this investigation low key but, thanks to Elliot Rockwell we now have a nickname for him, the 'child pose killer'. He targets young girls around the five to seven age group. He abducts them, kills them and leaves them posed where they will be easily found, hence the name. We are in communication with several other stations who have reported similar crimes spread across the country. We could have one killer or several, that's what we need to determine. Two girls on our patch so far, let's get him before he makes that three. Okay, you know what you need to do so let's get at it."

Patrick was a motivator; the room was buzzing with enthusiasm.

"Excellent, Patrick, thank you," acknowledged McGurn. "You already have a handpicked team for this but I'd like to offer you a little extra help."

McGurn made his way to where Meg was standing and pulled her forward. "Everyone, this is Meg Quinn, we've worked historic cases together. She's an asset to any team, so make her feel welcome."

Meg suddenly felt herself shrinking towards the floor, where she hoped a huge void would appear and swallow her up. Every eye in the room was surveying her. The women looked her up and down, scanning for flaws, and the men were mentally undressing her. She felt her face flush with colour at the unwanted attention.

"Welcome," said Patrick, extending a friendly hand. "You'll be with me today."

CHAPTER 13

Pollard Avenue was an extension of Harrow Lane, a wide, tree-lined suburb saturated by Victorian architecture. It was within walking distance of the coast and a short car journey to a handful of amenities and the shopping district, in the heart of Aberbarry.

Primrose Swann and Ewan Davis had taken opposite sides of the street to begin their house calls. For the most part the occupants had been sleeping, working or lived too far in proximity from the Pipers to know anything about them.

On the other side of the Pipers' house, the one unattached, lived Florence Darby. She was a delicate old lady with short white hair and eyes cloaked by cataracts. Florence stood no taller than a small child and just as petite. She rarely welcomed visitors and the arrival of a police officer was exciting.

Primrose was invited into the back parlour, which resembled an overgrown greenhouse. Plants and trees sprouted from every available space. A décor of jungle foliage, with leaves the size of umbrellas and vines hugging every inch of the garish floral backdrop.

"Sit down, make yourself comfortable, dear," hummed Florence as she fumbled with mugs and spoons and biscuits.

"What a remarkable room," commented Primrose, trying to think of an understated description.

"Thank you," replied Florence with a smile. "They're good company for a person who lives alone."

Primrose couldn't imagine how. A dog was good company, not an army of gigantic pot plants.

Florence finally took to her seat and began arranging a tea party of decorative China.

"Sugar, Officer?"

"Two, please."

"Milk or cream?"

"Milk's just fine."

"Biscuit, shortbread, Jammy Dodger or chocolate crunch?"

Primrose retrieved a thick slice of shortbread. "Now, Mrs Darby," she began.

"It's 'Miss', never found the time for a Mr Darby, but you can call me Florence," she interrupted.

"Well, Florence, I'm making enquiries about your neighbours, Eva and Edward Piper."

"Is that what they're called? Never did find the time to meet them."

The interview seemed futile. Florence never found the time to do anything other than tend her house plants. No wonder loneliness invaded her existence.

"So there's nothing you can tell me about them?"

"About who, dear?"

"The Pipers, your next-door neighbours."

It was becoming clear that Florence was in the flush of early dementia; her attention span was as diminutive as the old lady herself.

Primrose nibbled her way through the plate of biscuits and three refills of tea.

"Well, I best be going," she stated. "Lovely to meet you, Florence. By the way, have you any family in the area?"

Florence pondered for a moment, forcing the last dribble of tea through the strainer.

"I have a son, Marcus," she declared.

Primrose was astounded, assuming the lack of a Mr Darby had meant Florence was childless.

"Really? And where might I find him?"

"Don't look so shocked, Officer, I haven't always been a prisoner to vegetation," she mused, her senility suddenly overshadowed by meaningful conversation. "He was taken from just outside the front door. I was so exhausted, I fell asleep. When I went to bring him in he was gone, the pram was empty," she recalled with a matter-of-fact tone.

Before Primrose could comment the moment had passed and Florence's snapshot of clarity disappeared.

Constable Swann left the old lady busy in conversation with her greenery. She made a note of the son and moved to the next house.

***

On the other side of the road Constable Davis was entering the home of Celia Tucker under the guidance of Marjorie Kimble, her carer.

Inside the sanctuary of Celia's existence he took a seat on her freshly made bed. Marjorie hovered in the background, eager to interpret Celia's body language and incomprehensible attempt at speech.

"Good morning, Mrs Tucker, or can I call you Celia?" he began.

Celia nodded a positive response.

"I won't keep you long, I know you're not very well, but I just want to ask a few questions about your neighbours, the Pipers, who live just across the way."

Celia nodded again.

"Did you know Mr and Mrs Piper? Have you ever met?"

Celia reacted positively, a slight groan emerging from her silence.

"Can you remember when you last saw them?"

Celia raised her hand slightly and forced four fingers into the air.

"Four days ago?"

Celia shook her head.

"Four weeks?"

The response was positive.

"Okay, so you last saw them four weeks ago." He recorded the details in his notebook.

Celia must have been the last person to see them before their murder, as the pathologist had stated decomposition indicated they had been dead for around four weeks.

"They visit her. Well, Eva does... did," added Marjorie.

"And the last visit was when?" enquired Ewan.

"Probably four weeks, maybe a little more, I don't quite remember."

Constable Davis had now turned his attention to Marjorie as the questions continued to flow.

"Were they going away or off to visit family?" he queried.

"Yes, one or the other I think," Marjorie replied.

Celia was frustrated now, throwing her one good hand in the air, sending her sippy cup and its contents tumbling to the floor. Marjorie interpreted this action as Celia becoming overwhelmed by her visitor and brought the interview to an abrupt close.

Celia was inwardly screaming. The Pipers had no family. They were not going anywhere. Celia knew about the man who visited their home under the cover of darkness. She had the answers to the policeman's questions, but no one could see beyond the shell of the paralysed invalid and her inability to communicate.

***

Primrose had now exhausted her side of the avenue, meeting mostly empty houses. She crossed to Ewan's side as he disappeared from view.

She was standing at the top of a beautifully pebbled driveway, which led to a newly renovated home. The Victorian architecture had been defaced by contemporary metal window frames and double doors. Clipped topiary and dancing fountains, a plethora of garden lights and an intercom service completed the look.

Before she could reach for the buzzer a woman appeared, wrapped in a silk kimono, golden hair caressing her shoulders and smouldering emerald eyes. Primrose felt a little overwhelmed as she sucked in the portion of collapsed stomach oozing thoughtlessly between the buttons of her uniform.

"Good morning, Officer, what can I do for you?" The woman smiled, flashing a set of blinding veneers.

"Just making enquiries about your neighbours, the Pipers just across the road and about two houses down."

"The old couple in that obscenity they call a house?"

The woman was referring to the neglected exterior of the Pipers' home as she preened herself on the doorstep of her own obscenity.

"The Pipers," replied Primrose. "They were found murdered a couple of days ago."

The woman's fake tan paled slightly and for a moment Primrose thought a spark of empathy dulled her perfectly applied makeup, but her concern was not for the slaughtered victims but for her own safety.

"Oh my god, I need to call my alarm company, step up security if there's a murderer on the loose."

"Can I have your name, miss?" demanded Primrose with an air of hostility.

"I'm Sable Caine, Officer, you know...?"

Primrose looked at her with a blank expression, the name triggering no spark of recognition.

"Sable Caine," repeated the woman, "the movie star."

Primrose stifled a smirk. "I see. Sorry, I don't watch a lot of films."

"Me neither," giggled the woman, "unless I'm in it of course."

Primrose shuddered as the chill of an easterly wind whipped around her.

"Want to come in? You look frozen."

Primrose found Sable Caine irritating but her eagerness to peruse the lifestyle of a movie star was overpowering and she stepped inside.

Marble greeted her, on the floors, the staircase, even the furniture, muted neutrals of cream and grey.

She followed the billowing sleeves of the actress's gown into the living room. Velvet sofas, oversized cushions, fur rugs and crystal lighting. A glowing log fire captured behind glass and a gallery of explicit photographs of the actress. Suddenly Primrose realised that Sable Caine was none other than a porn star.

Primrose took her position in front of the fireplace, taking advantage of the warmth it emitted.

"Champagne, Officer?" questioned Sable, holding a gold-rimmed flute towards the constable.

Primrose declined politely.

"Now your neighbours, what can you tell me about them?"

"Not much, really, I haven't lived here long. Most seem hostile, keep themselves to themselves. I've met the guy next door and the couple over there." Sable pointed up the avenue; both were houses Primrose had already visited.

"What about the Pipers, the couple who were murdered?"

"I've not seen much of them, though I've seen their son coming and going occasionally. I wonder if I could bag their house at a really great price. It would be a great investment opportunity."

Primrose had zoned out of Sable's conversation except for the part that mentioned the Pipers' son. The DCI had said there was no family.

"How do you know it's their son?"

"Well, I assume he is. He lets himself in, he drove away in their car, who else would he be?"

Who else indeed!

"Can you describe him for me?"

Sable sipped at champagne, flicking through the snapshots of her self-obsessed mind, searching for an answer.

"Well he's average, I'd say, probably in his fifties or sixties. It's difficult to tell, really, I've only ever seen him at night."

Her description would have matched half the population of Wales, if not the entire United Kingdom.

"Any distinguishing features that you remember?"

"Shifty, looking around as if he's worried about being watched. Of course he doesn't know I've seen him. Discretion is my middle name."

Primrose wanted to chuckle, taking in the naked pictures once more. *Yes, looks like it*, she thought to herself.

***

Next door Ewan Davis was tapping at the last house on his list.

He could hear shuffling and a dog barking inside. He tapped again, this time slightly harder.

The door opened to reveal a middle-aged man, smartly dressed, wearing robust dark glasses and holding a white stick. A small terrier appeared at his feet, growling half-heartedly.

"Can I help you?" asked the man, his gaze directed slightly to the right of where Constable Davis stood. The man was obviously blind.

"Sorry to trouble you, sir, my name is Constable Davis."

"A policeman," stated the man with a giggle. "What have I done, Officer?"

"Nothing, sir, I'm just making enquiries about your neighbours, the Pipers."

"Ah yes, terrible business, you better come in."

Ewan stepped forward as the terrier made a bid for his ankle.

"That's quite enough, Rocky," scolded the man. "I'm so sorry, we don't get many visitors during the day so he's a little over protective."

"That's quite all right," replied the constable. "He's quite the security guard."

The blind man made his way down the hall and disappeared into the first door on his right. The house was immaculate.

"You live alone, sir?" questioned Davis, attributing the cleanliness to that of a feminine touch.

"Oh no, Officer, that would be quite impossible with my lack of sight. My brother lives with me, but he's out during the day at work."

"I see. It could be useful for me to speak with him as well, when it's convenient."

"Of course, leave your number on the coffee table and I'll ask him to get in touch. Now what did you want to know about the Pipers?"

Ewan realised that his usual pitch of 'have you seen or heard anything unusual?' wasn't appropriate for a man with no sight.

So he began with, "Did you know the Pipers at all?"

"No, not really. I don't venture out much these days; blindness has made me an unsociable bore, I'm afraid, and I'm a terrible host. Where are my manners, can I offer you some tea?"

Constable Davis would have loved to have said yes, but the man's affliction stopped him.

"How about I make you one?" he offered.

"That's very kind. I really can't say no, Officer, my home help has been and gone for the day. I can manage it myself but you'll be so much quicker if you don't mind, otherwise I'll wait until my brother gets home."

Ewan disappeared into the kitchen with Rocky observing his every move.

"Cups are top right, teabags in the caddy behind the teapot and spoons second drawer to the left," came the instructions from the living room.

Five minutes later the constable was serving tea.

"Wonderful, thank you."

"Have you lived here long Mr...?" enquired Davis.

"Stanmore, Felix Stanmore. Around a year, I'd say."

"Are you aware of the Pipers having any family?"

"I really couldn't say, Constable, though according to my home help who's a bit of a gossip, the answer is no. She keeps me abreast of the comings and goings in the outside world. She's become my eyes, if you will."

"That's fine, Mr Stanmore. I won't trouble you any longer."

Ewan thanked Felix for his company and bid him good day, leaving a contact number as promised.

CHAPTER 14

Tyla Cassidy was still missing.

Tully and Briggs had made initial contact with the traveller community and in particular her father, Reuben. He wasn't forthcoming with information, but DS Tully was certain the gypsy prince knew more than he was saying.

"We'll need a warrant to search the place," he suggested to his DCI.

"Don't you think the first thing they did after you left was get rid of any evidence knowing you're likely to return with a search team?" replied McGurn. "No, we need to put them under surveillance, Tully. Don't forget, it's only concrete evidence will put those bastards away."

Tully nodded. "I'll put Kramer and Hollis on it, sir."

"Not those buffoons. Isn't there anyone else?" groaned the DCI, showing his distaste for the unpopular duo.

"Sorry, sir, there isn't at the moment."

"Well swap them out as soon as you can," demanded McGurn, "and put someone on the boy, Joel, my money's on him being involved with the disappearance of his sister."

Tully nodded.

Primrose and Ewan updated the teams on information collected from the neighbours, though there wasn't an awful lot to go on. The best lead came from Sable Caine, who was certain the Pipers' evening visitor was their son.

"How do you feel about a couple of nights in a porn star's bedroom?" teased McGurn to Briggs, who flushed as the roar of testosterone emanated around the office. "She's agreed to us using her spare bedroom for surveillance."

"Whatever you need, sir," came his reply, a wry smile crossing his lips.

"A night at the porn star's house. What will the missus think about that?" mused Primrose.

"You can go too, Tully," declared the DCI. "I don't trust Briggs to keep his eyes on the job."

"Me either," giggled Swann.

Tully rubbed his hands together. "Certainly, sir, it will be my pleasure." He smirked sarcastically.

"In your dreams," added Davis. "From what I've heard she's out of your league."

"Jealous by any chance, Ewan?" teased DS Tully.

Constable Swann tossed a disapproving glance around the room, rolling her eyes at the sexual innuendos bouncing from one hormonal colleague to the next as they jeered and joked with Tully and Briggs.

"Honestly, you men never grow up. You've really not progressed in millions of years, you're still just a bunch of Neanderthals," declared Swann. "What's the purpose of this nighttime soiree, sir?"

"The purpose, Swann, is that most perpetrators return to the scene of the crime," scowled McGurn, decidedly unhappy with the cross examination.

"How many nights will the budget allow?" enquired Tully, still smiling.

"Two," snapped the DCI, "so don't get too comfortable, Sergeant you won't be there long."

🌳

When he returned home from work, he was less than excited by the police officer's visit, noticing the printed name card laying on the coffee table. The last thing he wanted was a return visit, especially if he had a fresh one in the basement.

Of course the expensive soundproofing was a more than adequate barrier, but if they wanted to take a look around, how would he explain the caged child?

As the colour of darkness painted the evening sky he disappeared into the basement beneath the house with one thing on his mind, blood.

***

Meg flitted between Aberbarry Police Station and Della's house. She read the recent statements taken from the neighbours and decided to embark on a spot of extracurricular investigation. When Della was sound asleep and Joel was locked in his room she left the house and entered the Pipers' through the back door using Della's spare key.

The house was creepy, the perfect setting for a scary movie with only the light of her torch to dissect the darkness.

The crime scene remained untouched; only the stained patch of carpet indicated where the Pipers had lain. Her mind flashed back, their gruesome remains suddenly appearing in front of her. She closed her eyes tight and they were gone.

Meg crossed from room to room in search of a breakthrough, but all three floors yielded nothing of significance. Only the basement remained unexplored.

She forced the stiffness of its door aside and descended the rickety staircase. *Why are basements so hostile?* she wondered, flashing torchlight from side to side. This basement, like most, was filled with unused objects, stored and forgotten, dusted with the cobwebs of passing time. A rusty bike, a broken rocking chair, an accumulation of empty paint pots and discarded furniture.

Sitting in the far corner almost hidden from sight behind a dismembered mannequin lay a small dust-covered suitcase. The locks were broken, an indication that the police search team had found it. At first glance, it appeared empty, but a faint jingle on closing it told Meg that it was not. She tugged at the lining and a small silver rattle dropped into sight. It was a baby's toy, tarnished with age but complete. A tiny blue ribbon decorated the handle embroidered with the letter 'M'.

CHAPTER 15

Two nights later DS Tully and DC Briggs moved into the front guest bedroom of Sable Caine's lavish home. They set up surveillance aimed at the Pipers' house ready to record the comings and goings of Pollard Avenue after dark.

The first few hours were unremarkable – a couple of taxi cabs, a boy on a bicycle, a dog walker who didn't bother to pick up and an elderly man with a small dog and white stick.

"That must be the guy from two doors down," revealed Briggs.

"What's he doing out at this time of night walking the dog?" questioned Tully.

"Think about it, doesn't matter to him whether it's day or night, does it? He's blind, you moron."

Sable caught their attention as she floated into the room with a tray of refreshments.

"Anything happening, boys?" she queried, hovering beside Davis with a mug of hot chocolate.

The constable of course, had no idea if anything was happening as he couldn't take his eyes off the voluptuous movie star.

"No, it's very quiet," replied Tully, watching the zombified Briggs floundering to find his voice.

"Gosh, it's exciting. What do you call it, a stakeout?" She giggled, stooping to take a look down the camera.

The waft of Chanel was overpowering, the flurry of feathers around the cuffs of her gown tickling Tully's cheek as she hovered beside him.

"Err... yes, that's right, a stakeout," gasped Tully as the outline of her breasts almost erupted from beneath their flimsy satin restraint.

"Who's that?" she mused, offering the camera to Tully.

"That's one of your neighbours, miss."

"Oh, really! Is he blind?"

Tully thought the answer was obvious but Sable needed reassurance.

"What a cute little dog he has," she commented, taking a further peek into the camera. At that moment a flash erupted as one of Sable's perfectly manicured acrylics touched the button accidentally.

Tully grabbed the camera abruptly. This wasn't good; their cover could be blown already. McGurn would be furious.

Sable left the room in a swirl of feathers.

He was taking a late-night stroll to clear his head. The child in the basement had been challenging. It was over now, though. She was finally quiet and still. It had been a relief to finish her, reclaim the silence she had so thoughtlessly disrupted. He'd left her to drain. Bodily fluids escaped after death, but a couple of days lying on the shower curtain would sort that. Blood dried relatively quickly and was easier to clean than leakage from other orifices. He supposed it was the downside of his sport. If only he'd taken up golf instead, it would be a far tidier and less hazardous option.

A sudden flash of light caught his attention. He looked towards the darkened houses around him searching for direction. A movement behind the curtains of the house with hideous windows gave him the answer. She was an adult movie star, he'd heard. Maybe she was filming her latest erotica, or was she filming him?

***

The following evening Tully and Briggs descended on Sable Caine's house for the second night. The gates were already open, heavy electric ones engraved with her initials. They parked at the side of the house hidden from view and waited for the gates to close, but they didn't.

Tully headed for the front door while Briggs unloaded the gear.

The bell rang inside but Sable didn't appear. Exasperated, Tully pulled out his phone and called her number. The faint sound of 'you sexy thing' by Hot Chocolate played out, but Sable didn't answer.

"She's forgot we're coming," stated Briggs, laden with heavy equipment. "She's probably relaxing in the bath."

But Tully didn't think so. He checked the door, it was locked. He patrolled the front of the house, then disappeared down the side towards the enormous conservatory at the back. The folding window that separated the house from the garden stood slightly ajar. He would have missed it had it not been for the hint of white lace material caught in its grasp.

Briggs set the gear aside and followed Tully into the house. It was quiet, still and bathed in subdued lamplight. A half-filled champagne flute rested on the coffee table beside an open magazine. The blinds were closed and the front door bolted. Tully climbed the staircase, the sole of his shoes tapping a tune on the marble as his pace quickened.

"Sable," he shouted.

He threw a glance towards Briggs as he stood at Sable's bedroom door. He pushed it gently and peered inside, flicking the light switch as he ventured forward.

"Oh my god," he uttered, holding a hand up to stop Briggs from following him but it was too late, he was in the room beside him, staring in disbelief at the brutalised body of Sable Caine. She was lying in the centre of her enormous bed, naked and dead. Her bed sheets were drenched in blood, their paleness now a deep shade of pink. She had been gutted from sternum to pelvis and left to perish.

"God, I hope she was dead when that was done to her," muttered Briggs, wearing a deathly pallor.

"Call this in, now!" commanded Tully.

CHAPTER 16

When Meg arrived at the station the next morning there was an urgency in her colleagues' demeanour. The buzz was not one of having caught a suspect, but of having gained another victim.

She learned about the death of Sable Caine at McGurn's emergency meeting.

McGurn was not his usual model of composure; his ruddy complexion had deepened and his cheeks puffed excessively as he struggled to control his breathing.

Tully and Briggs were skulking in a corner, having felt the wrath of the DCI moments earlier.

Patrick was in charge of the briefing as McGurn lingered in the doorway of his office.

"The Gov looks like he's about to have a heart attack," whispered Swann to Davis.

Patrick Grayson threw a stern glance in her direction.

"Right, listen up you lot. It seems that our surveillance operation on the Pipers' house is compromised. Last night Sable Caine, whose home we were using, was found murdered."

The room rumbled with shocked expressions and muttered opinions.

"Someone knew we were there and I suspect that someone is responsible for the slaughter of our hostess. Sable, like the Pipers, was butchered, split almost in two and left to drown in her own blood. What does this mean for us? Well it means we either have two killers on the loose or we are looking for one suspect responsible for all the murders, including those of the young children."

Patrick glanced at McGurn who nodded his agreement.

"What about Tyla Cassidy?" questioned Constable Davis.

"At this time we have nothing to suggest that Tyla Cassidy is another victim. She is still missing and we must treat her disappearance as a totally separate case, unless we have cause to believe otherwise."

"Are the Cassidys under surveillance?" questioned Meg.

Patrick hesitated before answering. "Kramer and Hollis were given that task as we have limited resources. The Pipers' house took priority, I'm afraid, but Tully and Briggs will take over from them today."

Meg was familiar with the answer. Difficult decisions and inadequate funds were at the heart of modern-day policing.

As the meeting came to a close Meg pulled Patrick to one side and revealed the baby rattle she had discovered in the Pipers' basement.

Patrick scowled disapprovingly. "What were you thinking, Meg?" he scolded.

"I was thinking we needed some evidence," she growled back.

"What, and this is it? An old-fashioned child's toy!"

"At least get it fingerprinted. If it's of no significance why was it hidden?"

"Look, send it to the lab. Now if you'll excuse me I have more pressing matters to attend to than a baby rattle."

Patrick left the office, a cloud of discontent hovering above his head.

***

Della was rapidly disappearing into the depths of depression. Meg feared she may find comfort in a bottle of painkillers and renew her previous relationship with addiction. Joel was spending more time with the Cassidys, which really didn't help. Meg felt inadequate. She toyed with the idea of going home, back to Fin and the loneliness of being a couple, but she couldn't leave Della. She couldn't bear the guilt of her turning back to drugs; she had no choice but to stay.

She fished Elliot Rockwell's number from her pocket and dialled.

"Hello, Elliot Rockwell."

His voice was refreshing, the tone soothing. She needed to laugh, to allow herself to escape from reality for just a couple of hours. Elliot was what she needed.

"You free for a drink tonight?" She held her breath waiting for his response, hoping he remembered her.

"Officer Castleton," he joked. "How lovely to hear from you."

Meg sighed with relief.

"How about dinner at Le Petite Brasserie? Come to the office for eight."

The line went dead. He hadn't waited for a response, but he knew she would accept.

***

Meg was partnered with DS Tully that afternoon, while Briggs kept eyes on Joel. They parked opposite the travellers' site tucked from view, waiting for signs of Reuben or Gerald Cassidy to emerge.

Conversation was sparse. Tully was still recovering from the discovery of Sable Caine's murdered body. His glazed expression told her so.

The silence was deafening and Meg felt obligated to pierce the quietude.

"Want to talk about it?" she began.

"About what?" came Tully's monotone reply.

"The murder."

"What's to talk about? She's dead."

"It's okay to feel like this, it never gets easier no matter how many murder scenes you attend."

"Attended a lot, have you?" Tully sounded sarcastic.

"My fair share," she replied hesitantly. "You heard of the Brightmarsh murders?"

"Course I have," sniffed Tully, making eye contact for the first time.

Meg stared at him. His eyes widened at the realisation of who she was and her connection with the gruesome event.

"You!" he gasped. "Meg Quinn, I hadn't realised, the change of name..."

"Castleton is my married name, though the DCI never remembers that fact."

"My god, how did you manage to get through that?" Tully was engaged now, the commonality between them having rallied his attention.

"Well you don't, really. You just do the best you can, but it's always there, haunting you, questioning your ability, your decisions. It will rule your life if you let it."

"I'm sorry," muttered Tully. "It's easy to wallow in your own self-pity."

"It is, that's why it's good to talk."

Tully mustered his emotions and conversation began to flow.

"Did you catch anything interesting on your camera the other night?" asked Meg.

"Can't imagine so, but it's with forensics, they're going through the footage."

"It's the tiniest of breakthroughs that can turn a case. Hopefully there will be something helpful."

Tully gripped Meg's arm suddenly.

"We're on the move," he announced as the silver Mercedes owned by Gerald Cassidy pulled into view. Reuben filled the passenger seat and an unknown figure lurked behind him, the face hidden from sight.

They swung onto the road and followed, staying two cars behind. The Mercedes bore left and headed for the A road that connected Llangoffey with Cwmdovey. It was hard to remain discreet as the traffic thinned and the Mercedes swung right and disappeared up a dirt track.

Tully drove past and took the next turning. The road was narrow and cosseted by overgrown hedges. A visual was impossible, but Tully kept driving. At a fork in the road he stopped and exited the car, climbing a nearby stile in the bushes to survey the area.

Meg opened the door. "Anything?"

Tully shook his head.

Suddenly a piercing sound cut the air and Tully dropped to the ground. Meg jumped from the car and raced to his side. Tully had been shot in the head; death had claimed him instantly.

"Oh my god," cried Meg as the flow of crimson pooled around her colleague's body.

She reached for her phone, no signal. She ran back to the car, grabbing the radio and screaming for help.

The radio spat and hissed as a fractured conversation took place. It seemed useless, her communication was incoherent.

She threw open the back car door and dragged Tully with every ounce of strength she could muster. In the distance the sound of screeching wheels alerted her that the silver Mercedes was powering towards them.

She heaved Tully onto the back seat and jumped behind the wheel. She spun the car around, reversing hastily in the confines of limited space and sped down the narrow lane, as the symbol of the silver Mercedes appeared in the rear-view mirror. The face of Gerald Cassidy lurched into sight as he nudged the back end of Tully's Frontera. The car jerked forward, throwing Meg onto the steering wheel like a rag doll. Undeterred, she placed her foot to the floor and prayed that nothing blocked her exit.

Eventually she reached the end of the lane and pulled erratically out onto the A road just missing the back end of a passing juggernaut. A mile down the road she spied a garage and pulled onto the forecourt, screeching to a halt. The silver Mercedes sailed past, its occupants staring menacingly after her. The third person was now visible – it was Joel Cassidy.

CHAPTER 17

That evening Meg drove to Aberbarry to meet up with Elliot Rockwell. Tully's death weighed heavy on her mind and she'd thought about cancelling the charming editor, but she needed his company now more than ever.

Elliot was waiting in the lobby of his newspaper building, bright eyed and smiling. He greeted her with a friendly hug and peck on the cheek.

"You okay?" he questioned as Meg embraced him tightly without warning.

"Sorry, I just needed that," she explained.

"Bad day?"

"You have no idea."

Elliot led her down the high street, across the playing fields where the white tent had once shrouded the murdered child, and onto a cobbled back street. They passed the glow of candlelit windows where a scattering of people dined in its ambience. Elliot pushed open the door and ushered her inside.

The place was charming, typically French with a hint of 'je ne sais quoi'.

"Bonsoir, Francois," conversed Elliot as though French were his native tongue.

"Bonsoir Monsieur Rockwell, I have your usual table for you," replied a smartly dressed maître d'. "I will send the sommelier over tout de suite."

Shades of purple velvets and gilded furniture, baroque-style mirrors and crystal chandeliers adorned the French eatery. Meg felt underdressed in her black jumpsuit and pumps, but Elliot assured her that she looked 'perfect'.

The menu was written in French for Elliot to translate, but the prices were most definitely in English. Meg had hoped to split the bill, but she couldn't afford more than the French onion soup, so she decided against it.

Elliot ordered a bottle of French champagne. It arrived in a bucket of ice and sat beside the table like an extra companion. Conversation flowed, as did the alcohol, and Meg was consumed by Elliot Rockwell's passion for life as the events of the day melted away.

Elliot had boarded at Eton, studied at Oxford, travelled the world and spoke two languages.

He was mesmerising, funny, kind and very handsome.

Fin had once held her attention in much the same way, charmed and loved her ferociously, but those days had become nothing more than distant memories of a life she no longer recognised. Was their marriage over? She wanted to remain positive, but the fact that she was enjoying the company of another man and longing for his touch told her otherwise.

Fin hadn't contacted her for the last couple of days. How was she to interpret that? Should she even bother to try?

As the restaurant emptied Elliot settled the bill, shook hands with Francois, thanked the servers and left a huge tip.

He took Meg by the hand as she negotiated the cobbled street having inhaled more than her body weight in champagne. She stumbled and faltered, sometimes purposely for Elliot to catch her, holding her against him with the scent of his cologne close enough to taste.

On the playing fields they stopped and embraced. A full moon was following them, spotlighting the ground where they stood. The sky was scattered with thousands of twinkling stars; the scene could not have been more perfect as Elliot folded her into his embrace and his lips made contact with hers.

The moment was brief. The distressed voice of a woman interrupted them. She was calling for help in the distance.

They followed the sound hastily, its urgency instantly sobering.

On the main street they emerged to find the woman sitting in the middle of the road. She was babbling and pointing, tears streaking her face as she gasped to form words.

Meg followed the direction of her finger. In the distance a figure lay across a wooden bench shadowed beneath the memorial honouring Aberbarry's fallen soldiers.

"Stay with her," ordered Meg as she crossed the street leaving Elliot to console the woman.

Nearing the bench it became clear that the figure belonged to a child, who was lying fully clothed, and unmoving.

Meg's stomach began to churn, the taste of champagne clawing at her throat. The hint of a pigtail confirmed her suspicion. The child had been placed on her side with her face towards the memorial. Meg approached praying that the child was merely sleeping, but the sight of blood dripping between the weathered timber and pooling on the paved stone beneath told her she was wrong.

"God no, not another one," she muttered to herself.

CHAPTER 18

Meg's discovery of another child was shocking, as was the death of DS Tully. The station was shrouded in sympathy as colleagues, especially his longstanding partner Briggs, fought to digest the news. The culprit was Gerald or Reuben Cassidy, Meg was certain, but proving it was another matter entirely. Hard evidence was needed when the Cassidys were involved; that meant catching them in the act or finding something so damning they would certainly be found guilty.

McGurn was beside himself.

"What the hell is happening in this town?" he bellowed. The station shook with the ferocity of his emotions. He was deeply frustrated, the burden of guilt he carried almost unbearable. He was not in the habit of leaving cases unsolved, but time was ticking and his retirement was approaching.

"Right, people, listen up," he demanded. "As you've probably already heard and if not then you're hearing it now, another child has been found. Same MO as the others except that this time the body wasn't kept after death. This child was still warm, death had only just taken her, the killer could still have been in the vicinity as Quinn approached her. She bears the same horrific wound, same knife according to pathology. The question is, what makes her different from the others? Why was the killer so keen to dispose of her? Why did he not follow his usual pattern?"

"Maybe he's getting sloppy," came the first answer.

"Maybe we've got him riled," came the second.

"Maybe we're closing in," came the third.

"Maybe he got disturbed," came the last.

McGurn smiled. "Maybes don't solve a case, good old-fashioned police work does. I need boots on the ground. People solve crimes, nosey, interfering busybodies. Swann, Davis, revisit the neighbours. If they're not home find out where they are and go after them. I want to know everything about everyone who lives on Pollard Avenue whether you think it's relevant or not."

Swann and Davis nodded in unison.

"Meg, Patrick, I want you to revisit the location where DS Tully was shot. What were the Cassidys doing out there, where were they going and why? I know it will be difficult, Meg, but you're the only person who can lead us in the right direction on this."

Meg agreed. Losing DS Tully was awful, but their relationship was in its infancy, they hadn't formed the bond that long-term partners experience after years together in the field.

Patrick took the wheel and followed Meg's directions. They reached the lane where the silver Mercedes had turned and did the same. The narrow road eventually broadened, opening out onto an expanse of farmland with unkempt fields on both sides.

"Stop here, please," said Meg. She left the car and stood at a low-level fence taking in the view from all directions.

"What you looking for?" queried Patrick.

"There." Meg pointed, her finger tracing the hedge line on the far side of the field, stopping at the smallest gap in the bushes. "That's where Tully was standing when he was shot."

"Okay, so Cassidy was standing right about here, I'd say. He must have had a scope to hit Tully so accurately from this range," declared Patrick.

"You thinking a rifle?"

"Most definitely. Let's carry on up this road and see where we get to. Something brought the Cassidys up here, I want to know what."

They followed the line of the road for another mile or so, until the roof of a farmhouse teased their curiosity.

"I think we should park up here and walk. If anyone's home the sound of a car approaching will alert them to our presence," suggested Meg.

Patrick agreed and they abandoned the car behind a couple of ageing oak trees, out of sight of the road.

The ground was soggy, saturated with potholes and soaked through their flimsy footwear but they soldiered forward. Over the fence they climbed beneath the cover of a dilapidated outbuilding. The house was silent. No animals roamed the fields nearby and no dogs barked at their presence.

"I know you're not adverse to a little danger, but stick close. If anyone is home they could be armed," Patrick advised.

They crossed from building to building, stopping, waiting and listening. No signs of life erupted from within the farmhouse and no vehicles graced the yard.

Patrick headed for the front windows, peeping quickly inside, then ducking out of sight and crawling to the next. Meg followed closely. At the side of the house Patrick stopped. "I'm pretty sure the place is empty," he declared.

Meg had been here before, standing at the door of Molecatcher Farm listening for signs of life, except the life inside had been extinguished. "I think we should take a look inside," she proffered.

Patrick agreed and they headed to the rear of the farmhouse. The door to a boot room opened with ease. Patrick edged inside; from there he found the kitchen. Mouldy remnants of half-eaten sandwiches had taken root on the kitchen table, decaying fruit and empty packets of sweets.

"Looks like someone's been here, but not for a while," suggested Patrick. "You keep looking down here and I'll check upstairs."

Meg headed cautiously to the next room, the living room, cosy and welcoming in a crowded sort of way. A log fire had disintegrated in the hearth with a basket of kindling waiting patiently beside it. Large armchairs padded with cushions and throws, a heavily patterned rug and old-fashioned lanterns completed the scene. Empty coffee mugs and biscuit crumbs sat beside a photograph of an elderly couple. Meg took a closer look; the faces looked familiar, could it be that this was a picture of Eva and Edward Piper in their younger days?

Suddenly she was distracted as the voice of Patrick Grayson echoed down the stairs.

"Meg, come look at this."

Meg raced to find him standing in the doorway of a small bedroom.

She peered inside. On the floor lay ten sleeping bags, child-sized and empty. Meg paced the room stepping between the makeshift beds carefully.

"What does this mean, Patrick?" She grimaced.

Patrick sighed. "It means nothing good, that's for sure. Could be child trafficking or worse."

Meg realised, even though Patrick didn't say it out loud, a paedophile ring.

"Oh my god, poor babies." She slipped her hand beneath the nearest bag and flipped it over. A stain of urine patterned the inside, the mark of fear, the symbol of insecurity.

"We need to get forensics up here," suggested Patrick.

"I agree, although if we want to catch the bastards responsible white suits and sniffer dogs are going to alert them. Shouldn't we stake out the place in case they come back?"

"That's for McGurn to decide. I'm not paid enough to make those decisions."

They were about to leave the room, when Meg noticed the tip of a soft toy caught in the zip of the sleeping bag nearest to the door. She lifted it into view; it was a small giraffe wearing a red bow tie.

"Tyla..." Her heart rate quickened and a knot of emotion tightened inside, as she imagined the innocent face of the little girl and how afraid she must feel.

"If that belongs to Tyla we have no choice than to get a team in," declared Patrick.

Downstairs Meg waited for a decision from the DCI. She showed the photograph of the elderly couple to Patrick.

"No way, the Pipers!"

"Yes, I think so," agreed Meg.

"Do you think this is their house? Are they involved in trafficking somehow?" Patrick's mind was buzzing with questions.

"Well that's what we need to find out," replied Meg.

CHAPTER 19

The office was in a state of fervour. McGurn had recruited extra officers from a neighbouring town to help with the growing workload. Every inch of space was filled with the buzzing of voices and the beavering of eager young constables desperate to make a positive impression.

McGurn called a meeting, which resembled more of a school assembly than a police briefing.

"How old are some of these?" asked Swann, eyeing the spotty-faced rookies, who seemed young enough to be her grandchildren.

"You're getting old," Davis replied, for which he received a brisk elbow to the ribs.

"Right, troops, your attention please," shouted McGurn as the hum of conversation muted. "We've lots to get through. Patrick, if you please..."

Patrick took the lead, summarising the discovery made at the farmhouse, the toy giraffe and the photograph of the Pipers.

"Forensic teams will be working around the clock to find us the evidence we need to tie the Cassidys to this place. The sleeping bags are being analysed for DNA in the hope of identifying the children they belong to and we are trawling the database for recent reports of missing children in the hope of finding and bringing a modicum of news to their families. We need to know what part the Pipers played in any of this, if indeed they did. Did we get anything on who owns the property?" He glanced towards a fresh-faced constable wearing far too much makeup and unsavoury green nail polish.

"Yes, sir, the property belongs to a Marcus Piper."

"So there is a son, just like Sable said," declared Briggs.

"Do we have a current address for him?" demanded Patrick.

"No, sir, he doesn't seem to exist," replied the constable with the flash of a smile.

"He's dead?"

"No, sir. Well, he's not been registered so if he is."

"His birth should be registered."

"No, sir, it isn't, not by that name anyway."

"So we're looking for the invisible man, are we?" Patrick was agitated by the lack of information.

At that point Briggs received a phone call. "Thanks, I'll tell her." He searched for Meg in the crowd of new faces. "That was Steve in pathology, results on a baby's rattle?" he queried.

"Yes, what did he say?" begged Meg eagerly.

"The prints are a match with the Pipers."

McGurn smiled and nodded his admiration towards Meg. "Good work, Quinn. So we have confirmation that the Pipers did have a child and he owned the farmhouse. So what's the connection between him and the Cassidys? Find me the answers, people."

Patrick dispersed the gathering with a wave of his hands.

McGurn beckoned Meg and Patrick to follow him to his office.

"Just thought I'd let you know that with DS Tully gone I've managed to secure a temporary replacement. He's a secondment from out of town, arriving on Friday. That's all."

"If the Pipers had a son wouldn't we have found some photographs or paperwork about him in their house?" questioned Meg.

"Ordinarily you'd think so, but I don't think we're dealing with ordinary in this case," replied Patrick. "Think about it, where did you find the rattle?"

"Hidden in the lining of an old suitcase."

"Exactly, that tells me that the Pipers wanted to keep their son a secret. Why else would they hide the only object that confirmed his existence?"

Patrick was right.

"I think I'll run a check on missing children in the fifties and sixties just in case something turns up," declared Meg.

"Good idea, now I've got to run Charlie has the photos for me to look at from Tully's camera."

***

Back at Della's, Meg waited impatiently for confirmation that the toy giraffe belonged to Tyla. She couldn't divulge the recent find to her friend for fear of giving her false hope or spiralling her depression out of control at the thought of Tyla being trafficked or even worse.

Joel wasn't home again and Della seemed surprisingly upbeat for once. Meg hoped the sudden change was not the responsibility of drug use, but she decided to embrace the new mood and they spent the evening together.

Over dinner and a glass of chardonnay conversation turned to minor interrogation.

"Did you know the Pipers had a son?" Meg casually informed.

"No, really. They never talked about a son, not that I talked to them that much."

"So you never saw a man visiting the house?"

"Can't say I did. The Pipers were very private people, unsociable I suppose you'd say."

"Did they know you had children?"

"Well they must have heard them playing out the back, but I never formally introduced them, why?"

"Oh, no particular reason, just trying to get a feel for the type of people they were."

"Paedo Piper," blurted out Della with a giggle, "that's what my grandad called Edward."

Meg's ears pricked. "Really? How so?"

"Oh, I don't know. My grandparents lived here as long as the Pipers, in fact, apart from Miss Darby and Celia Tucker, the Pipers and my grandparents were the original neighbours. My grandfather had the notion that Edward Piper was 'into children' as he put it, but not in a good way," informed Della. "Maybe he'd seen or heard something over the years to make him think that."

Meg at that point was wishing Della's grandfather was still alive and able to elaborate his thoughts on Mr Piper.

"Anyway, tell me about your date last night?" Della grinned, changing the subject and pouring another two large glasses of wine.

"It wasn't a date, just a chat, but it was nice, he was nice." Meg blushed slightly. She played with the ring on the third finger of her left hand, the gold band that bound her in marriage to Fin. She hadn't thought about him much recently, if at all, and a pang of guilt tugged at her conscience.

"So you seeing him again?"

That was the question Meg didn't want to answer mainly because she didn't know. Elliot had been texting her all day; nothing passionate, just platonic with a hint of flirtation.

"Let me rephrase that, would you like to see him again?"

Meg gulped at the wine. She wasn't used to being put on the spot like that, not where her personal life was concerned.

"Well I'm still married, Della, I'm hardly going to fix me and Fin by chasing another guy, now am I?"

"I think the question is, can you and Fin be fixed?"

Della was right; three years of marriage fraught with disappointment and haunted by the trauma of tragedy and loss. Was it possible to come back from that?

"I can only see when I get home," she sighed. "Only time will tell."

At that moment her phone beeped, a message from Patrick – 'giraffe belonged to Tyla'.

Della's face questioned Meg's sudden and solemn expression, but Meg hadn't the heart to break the news. Della was in such a good place for the first time since she had arrived, she couldn't bring herself to spoil the evening. She would break the news tomorrow.

"Just a work thing," she confirmed, refilling Della's glass. "Now time for you to tell me about the men in your life, Ms Warren."

"That's easy, there aren't any, well, except for Joel and even he's not here much now." Della scanned the kitchen, focusing on the back door in the hope that at any moment Joel would enter.

"Yes, where is he these days?" questioned Meg.

"With his father and the Cassidy clan. I think he likes being with them more than me. Can't blame him, I suppose I haven't been much of a mother lately."

"Stop criticising yourself, Della. He should be here supporting you, for God's sake."

"That would be nice, but for a while I'd forgotten I had two children, I was so focused on Tyla. I've pushed him away without meaning to."

Della went quiet, her eyes glazing with the onset of tears.

"We're going to find her, Della," comforted Meg, taking hold of her hand across the table.

The brief silence that followed was welcome as each woman disappeared into their own thoughts. Only the voice of Della's favourite artist filled the interval.

Suddenly Della jumped from the table and disappeared into her pantry, reappearing with a third bottle of wine. Meg glanced at the clock. It was after midnight, sleep was calling, but Della was desperate for company and the cork had popped.

"Can I ask you a personal question?" slurred Meg, suffering the effects of alcohol for the second night that week.

"Of course, Meg, ask me anything."

"Why did you give Tyla the Cassidy name, why not Warren?"

"Well that's easy, I wanted her to have the same last name as her brother, so that no one asked awkward questions. You know how other kids can be."

It was a fair enough answer and the reasoning made sense, but Reuben Cassidy, really, what was she thinking?

"Fair enough. Has there been anyone else apart from Reuben and the one-night stand? I mean, anyone substantial?"

Della pondered for so long that Meg thought she had fallen asleep with her eyes open.

"Yes, there was a special someone once, but I messed it up like I always do. I met him in a nightclub, we had a couple of dates, he was kind and so handsome..."

Della drifted away momentarily.

"So what happened?" begged Meg, shaking Della into consciousness.

"He found out I had a habit and that was it, I never saw him again."

Della's head hit the table. This time she had disappeared into an inebriated coma. Meg cushioned her head and tossed a blanket around her shoulders, turned out the light and staggered to bed.

CHAPTER 20

Daylight hit Meg's face with blinding ferocity. She forced an eyelid open and searched for the time. She lay fully dressed, waking in the position she had unwittingly adopted the night before. The taste of stale wine soured her breath and the woodpecker drilling at her temples was relentless.

She managed a coffee before expelling it violently. A shower and change of clothes made her presentable. She tossed a packet of painkillers into her bag and headed for the station.

🌳

He'd been away for a couple of days, it had been heaven without him. No unreasonable demands, no desperate urges, just Rocky and himself to please.

The last time had been a fiasco. He cringed at the thought of the botched disposal of his latest kill. He'd left the body on a bench in the centre of town. He hadn't cleaned her or dressed her, he hadn't even posed her. Usually he managed the child after death, but he had been in a mood, and practically salivating to perform the reckless act himself.

"Throw caution to the wind for a change," he had said.

That's all well and good, but he didn't have to clean up afterwards. Sudden deviations from the plan without due consideration of the consequences could lead to discovery. He'd got his way this time but going forward there could be no more surprises. Control was the key to their success, at least if he wasn't left to make the decisions.

The sound of a door opening caught his attention.

***

Meg reached the office just as the briefing was about to begin. The throbbing in her head had subsided temporarily with the aid of painkillers, but the gastric turmoil was unrelenting.

Patrick was posting photographs on the evidence board. McGurn was unusually absent.

"Right, these are the proofs from DS Tully's camera from the night before Sable Caine was murdered. Most are of little consequence; the boy on a bike wearing a hoodie has been eliminated from enquiries, the man walking his dog is a neighbour. As you can see he's blind, so I'm pretty sure we can rule him out too. This last one captures a hand, here just to the left of the picture. This is a blown-up image of that hand. What I'm interested in is the watch. It pre-dates the First World War, so it's pretty ancient, like you, Davis," joked the DI as raucous laughter plagued the room momentarily. "There aren't many of these watches in circulation today, it's rare and I want to talk to the man whose wrist it is decorating."

"Is that our man then, sir?" questioned Swann.

"I'm not saying that, but I want to eliminate him. He's outside the Pipers' house, maybe just taking a stroll, but the time on the image is 1:10am. What's he doing out and about at that time?"

"Maybe he's an insomniac," a voice shouted from the back of the room.

"Yes, thank you," scolded Patrick. "Any news on the Pipers' son? Did you pull the births, Katie?"

The room erupted with bawdy howls and whistles as DI Grayson let slip the constable's name.

"Grow up, you lot," he smirked.

"I have a list of names, none of a Marcus Piper, but I'm processing each one and eliminating those that aren't relevant. It's going to take some time though, sir, it's a laborious task."

"Okay, let me know if you find anything that might be relevant. I'll see if I can get you extra help, but don't count on it."

As the briefing closed Patrick ushered Meg into the DCI's office.

"What's going on?"

"We're meeting the new DS. McGurn's with him now, won't be long."

Meg swallowed three cups of water and prayed they would stay in situ.

"Heavy night?" smiled Patrick.

"Do I look that bad?" queried Meg.

"Let's just say I can spot a hangover at thirty paces."

The door of the office swung open and McGurn stepped into view.

"I'd like you to meet our temporary DS, Finlay Castleton," he announced.

Meg almost sank to the floor, the blood drained from her face and the headache returned, not to mention the surge of gastric content that erupted at the back of her throat, as she struggled to force it back down.

"You all right, Quinn? You look a bit peaky," questioned the DCI.

"Surprise!" revealed Fin with a glint in his eye.

"Am I missing something here? Do you two know each other?" enquired McGurn.

"Know each other, sir? Meg is my wife."

It was McGurn's turn to pale as he glanced between the couple.

"Well, personal lives are left at home," he spluttered, "you're both here to do a job, so let's be professional about this," sensing the air of tension between them.

In the corridor out of earshot of her colleagues Meg questioned, "What are you doing here?"

"I've been seconded for as long as I'm needed," Fin replied as if the opportunity had merely found him.

"You, of all the DS's in the country just happen to be seconded to this very place?"

"Aren't you pleased to see me?"

"A little warning would have been nice, Fin. I haven't heard from you for days and then you just turn up like it's the most normal thing in the world," said Meg, skilfully dodging the question.

"I expected a better welcome. Besides, this is when we're at our best, working together, solving crimes."

Meg felt exasperated, but Fin was here now and McGurn expected professionalism.

"Where are you staying? There isn't room at Della's," knowing full well that she was lying.

"Don't worry, I've booked in at The Great House B&B in town."

Patrick grabbed Meg's attention. "You free for a spot of door knocking? Davis and Swann have been put on the Marcus Piper investigation for a couple of days."

Meg nodded gratefully. "Absolutely, let's go."

CHAPTER 21

He was relentless, his insatiable lust for blood becoming almost uncontrollable. A couple of days away had stoked his desire. The presage of capture was imminent unless he mastered his thirst. There could be no more children for a while, or they would have to move house again and he was getting too old to manage the upheaval of such an event. The police presence was multiplying; two murders on the same street had to raise questions and neighbours would be top of the suspect list.

He visited the basement, hiding the cage beneath the cover of blankets. He folded the children's clothes, the ones he had cut from their bodies after death, patterned with the residue of dried blood. They needed burning, he'd light a fire tonight and dispose of them. The smell of bleach had faded, muted by the incense and candles that permanently resided there.

He heard the dog bark. Someone was at the door.

***

DC Briggs had been partnered with the new DS. A tall, ruggedly handsome man with dark hair and friendly demeanour. The plethora of age lines that creased his face were not the result of age, but of someone whose life had been touched by a trauma so great it left an indelible impression. Behind the smiling façade Briggs detected loneliness and sorrow; he knew the signs, he'd met them before.

"Want to drive?" Briggs offered as the two men headed for the car park of Aberbarry Police Station.

"Why not?" came the reply. "Although you'll have to give me directions, I've never been down this way before."

"Not a problem. We're heading to Llangoffey, follow the signs and I'll let you know when we get closer. We're visiting a rather unsavoury family, infamous in these parts, the Cassidys."

"Travellers?" questioned Fin.

"How d'you know?"

"Just a hunch."

As the signs for Llangoffey dwindled Briggs directed their journey down a couple of country lanes, emerging onto a dual carriageway with a turn three miles further on the left.

A sprawling settlement of mixed caravans and mobile homes stretched across several acres of field. They approached the gated driveway and waited.

"What's the plan? Are we here for a friendly chat or do we need to come down heavy?" queried Fin.

"Let's see how it plays out. They're a wily bunch, so stay on your toes. Anything can happen when you're dealing with Gerald Cassidy. He shot my partner a couple of weeks ago."

"You looking for proof?"

"The firearm will be long gone, just want him to know that his card is marked."

Fin nodded as the gates to the infamous Cassidy empire swung open.

***

"Good morning, sir. Sorry to bother you," began Meg, introducing herself and DI Grayson to the blind man who answered the door. A small terrier fretted beside him, sniffing at their ankles as they stepped inside.

"No bother at all, Officers, can I offer you some tea?"

Grayson shrugged, mouthing silently, 'Is he capable of such a task considering his disability?'

Meg ignored his concern and accepted.

The man felt his way around the kitchen, perfectly adept at the tea-making process, a task he had obviously performed many times before.

In the comfort of easy chairs armed with tea and biscuits, Meg began. "As you know there have been two murders in the neighbourhood recently."

"Quite so, a most terrible business. This has always been such a quiet part of town, never so much as a noise complaint before. What is the world coming to when you're not safe in your own home?"

"Absolutely, sir. I do hope you have security and lock your doors even during the daytime, especially if you live here alone," advised Meg.

"As I explained to your colleagues previously, I live with my brother. He's fastidious where security is concerned, so no need to worry, Officer."

"Obviously you've been visited before, this is just a follow-up since the murder of Ms Caine. Is there anything you can tell us about your neighbours that might give you cause for concern?"

"Nothing I can think of. I'm not a terribly sociable person for obvious reasons." He clutched at the white stick positioned beside his leg.

"It must be quite lonely for you, if you don't mind my saying," added Patrick, who had been quietly observing the well-spoken, pleasant gentleman.

"Well, I have a cleaner who visits and of course, my brother is here most evenings."

"Do you ever venture out alone?"

"Yes, sometimes if I'm feeling a little claustrophobic I'll take a late-night stroll with Rocky here."

"Well thank you for your time and the tea," mused Meg. "We will show ourselves out."

"Not at all, Officers, I welcome the company."

"One last thing, sir." Patrick paused in the doorway. "Have we spoken to your brother?"

"I'm pretty sure so. The last officer left a number for him to call and I'm certain he will have carried out the request."

***

Gerald Cassidy was waiting as they pulled alongside his ornately decorated home, a wry smile across his lips.

"To what do I owe the pleasure, again!" He smirked knowingly.

Briggs remained calm, but beneath the outward composure an angry storm was raging uncontrollably and the urge to punch Gerald full in the face was overwhelming.

Briggs jerked forward, the impulse reaching its climax. Fin placed a steady hand on his shoulder. "I've got this," he muttered, stepping protectively in front of the DC.

"Gerald Cassidy, I'm DS Castleton," he began.

"You're the replacement," grinned the traveller.

"I'd like to ask you a few questions about your whereabouts last Tuesday."

Gerald shouted for Reuben who appeared beside his father, a younger, but equally arrogant version.

"The officer wants to know where we were last Tuesday, son."

Reuben spat out, "We were at the races, Pa, don't you remember?"

"That's right, the races, memory's not what it used to be."

"You have someone who can corroborate this?" commanded Fin.

"Yeah, all of these..."

Fin turned to face a dozen intimidating stares, as family and friends of Gerald Cassidy had gathered to endorse his story.

Fin continued unperturbed. "Do you own a firearm, Mr Cassidy?"

"Let me think now, do I own a firearm?" he retorted smugly.

"It's a simple enough question. Do you or do you not own a firearm?"

"I used to," growled Cassidy.

"What type was it?"

"The type that could do a lot of damage." Gerald stared between Fin and Briggs, a threatening undertone to his answer.

"This your car?" Briggs piped up, finally composed enough to ask a question.

"It's mine actually," scowled Reuben.

"Mind if I take a look inside?"

"Got a warrant?" His cockiness gained momentum.

"No, but I can easily get one," replied Briggs.

"You do that then, Officer."

At that point Fin and Briggs did the sensible thing and retreated from the Cassidys' property. The situation was becoming volatile and neither officer was well enough equipped to take on the aggressive group of men waiting in readiness for Gerald to signal their requirement.

"Nasty bunch," declared Fin as he drove away to abusive shouts and gestures.

"I want to nail the bastard, but you see what we're up against, they close ranks. It's going to be an impossibility."

"Nothing's impossible, Briggs. Did you get the reg. number?"

Briggs nodded.

***

"Nice man," commented Meg as they left the blind man's property. "You were pretty quiet though."

"Yeah, you had it under control and I thought he'd open up more to a woman," replied Patrick.

"That's a sexist comment, DI Grayson," mused Meg.

"Not at all, it's a known fact that most men like to be interviewed by a woman. What's sexist about that?"

"Lovely home to say two men live there," added Meg.

"Now who's being sexist?"

"It's a known fact that most men don't keep house like a woman," she giggled.

"I noticed his watch. A cheap knock-off, I'd say."

"So we can cross him off our list of suspects then?" mused Meg.

The next house belonged to a tiny elderly woman, who from a distance could easily have been mistaken for a child.

Meg checked the list. "Florence Darby?"

"Yes, dear, can I help you?"

Florence was way too trusting and invited the strangers at her door to step inside without asking for any form of identification.

Meg explained the purpose for their visit and Patrick revealed his badge.

They followed the spritely little woman into her parlour, as she called it.

"Wow," exclaimed Patrick, surveying the jungle of pot plants and foliage that invaded the room.

Florence didn't ask if anyone wanted tea, she provided it without a word, along with a slice of Victoria sponge freshly baked that morning.

"Tuck in," she prompted, placing two enormous wedges of cake in front of them.

Florence babbled on about her plants and the recipes she had inherited from her grandmother, one being for the sponge that they were now enjoying.

"Ms Darby," interrupted Meg between mouthfuls of the delicious gateau.

"Florence, please."

"Florence, we're here because of the murders that happened recently, the one next door and now the one across the road from you."

"Yes, dear," uttered the old woman, seemingly oblivious to the recent occurrences.

"Do you live alone, Florence?" began Patrick.

Florence was attentive now. The handsome man with the piercing blue eyes had spoken and he held her in his gaze.

"Yes, it's just me and my babies, of course." Florence waved a hand around the room indicating the overgrowth of greenery being the babies she referred to.

"Do you have security, an alarm, dead locks?"

Florence appeared nonplussed, a vacant expression crossing her face.

"Never mind, I'll take a look before we leave," Patrick offered. "Do you venture out much?"

The elderly woman pondered for a while before replying as if she were performing mental arithmetic, "1987," she replied, "was the last time I left this house."

There was solemnity about her tone, but she smiled pleasantly as though the walls of her imprisonment were perfectly adequate.

Patrick glanced at Meg and raised his eyebrows.

"Do you often get visitors?" queried Patrick sympathetically.

"The window cleaner once a month, my grocery delivery each week and my cleaner," she replied. "More tea, dear?"

Florence Darby was hostage to a debilitating phobia and for that reason Patrick and Meg accepted further refreshments.

"Any chance I can use your bathroom?" begged Meg, feeling the effects of her fourth cup of tea.

"Of course, dear, up the stairs first door on the left."

The interior of Florence Darby's house was host to untouched authentic Victorian mouldings; the staircase had been patched and the heavily patterned carpet was threadbare in places. A deep green colour washed the walls and a gallery of sepia photographs hung in heavy frames at perfectly executed intervals.

The bathroom was thankfully in keeping with modern-day ablutions. A glass cabinet hung above the basin brimming with medication. The scent of lavender puffed from an automated air freshener and frilly curtains hung at the window. Meg washed her hands and started downstairs admiring the album of family portraits along the way. She stopped at the bottom of the stairs where the picture of a small boy hung. His was the only coloured photograph, indicative of a different era to the others.

"Here she is," declared Patrick as Meg entered the room. "We'll be on our way, Florence, but I'll check your locks first."

Florence followed them down the hallway like an excited school girl, as Patrick flicked at the bolts and catches on the back of her front door.

"Who's the little boy?" Meg queried.

Florence turned to look, walking closer, and touched the frame with a bony finger.

"That's my child," she sighed.

"You have a son?"

"Had a son," she corrected.

"Might I ask what happened?" ventured Meg cautiously.

"He disappeared from his pram in the garden."

"He was only a baby?"

"Almost three, dear, hard work at that age for one person. I'd fallen asleep and when I went to bring him back in the pram was empty." She sighed thoughtfully.

"You have no idea what happened to him? Were the police not involved?"

"Oh yes of course, dear, but they could find no trace of him. It's like he disappeared into thin air."

"Would you like me to try and find out for you?"

For a moment the old woman's eyes sparkled with anticipation. "You can do that?"

"Technology has come a long way, Florence. Nowadays there are very few people who can vanish without reason. At least let me try?"

Florence gripped Meg's hand gratefully. "Thank you, dear."

"You've got pretty good security, Ms Darby," added Grayson, "now keep this locked at all times."

Florence nodded and secured the lock as they left.

CHAPTER 22

Meg didn't return to the station that afternoon but headed back to Della's. She didn't want to bump into Fin again, she was still reeling from his surprise arrival and she needed to inform her friend about the discovery of Tyla's toy giraffe.

Della was in the kitchen with Joel watching TV.

Meg wanted to catch her alone, just in case McGurn's hunch was correct and Joel was somehow involved with Tyla's abduction.

She parked herself at the kitchen table and pulled out a laptop.

"I hear Fin's in town," announced Della.

"How do you know?" queried Meg, surprised by Della's knowledge.

"Joel told me."

Meg glanced at Joel with a questioning expression.

"He was at the campsite earlier," he declared.

"How did that go?" she scoffed with an air of belligerence.

"Dad and Grandad scared him off good and proper," came the reply.

Meg wanted to retaliate but Joel was a naïve teenager and blood was thicker than water.

She tapped away, inserting Florence Darby's name into her browser. Her phone pinged with a message from Elliot – 'free tonight?'

This was awkward, two men vying for her affections; the first should have them already and the second, well, there should never have been a second, but there was.

Della jumped from the sofa and switched on the kettle.

"Fancy a brew?"

"No!" answered Meg abruptly. "Sorry, I just couldn't stand to see another cup of tea today."

"Something stronger then?" queried Della, waving an unopened wine bottle in the air.

"Just the one then," cautioned Meg, recalling the aftermath of the night before.

Della sat beside her. "Was that Elliot?"

Meg nodded meekly.

"What are you going to do?"

"Della, I have no idea. Fin showing up like this has just confused me even more. I'm terribly angry with him for not discussing it with me first, but then part of me is pleased to see him, kind of like that old slipper feeling. Comfortable, if you know what I mean?"

"Well I suppose you're going to have to decide whether the old slipper has fallen apart and whether it's time to get new."

They clinked glasses and drank.

"Hey, why are you looking up Florence Darby?" asked Della, taking note of the name on the screen.

"Apparently she had a son."

"That's right," Della confirmed. "My brother used to look after him, a long time ago."

"Your brother?" queried Meg, trying desperately to retrieve a memory of Della's sibling. "I thought you were an only child?"

"I sort of was. Adrian is fifteen years older than me, I was a complete surprise. Mum thought it was menopause and it turned out to be yours truly."

"Can you remember anything about him, the child I mean?"

"Not personally, only snippets of things I heard from Adrian. He did a spot of babysitting for pocket money."

"Must have been hard for an unmarried mother in those days," commented Meg.

"Not that much easier now," replied Della, recalling the conversation that had taken place with the police officers regarding Tyla's father.

"You know she hasn't left that house in decades," informed Meg.

"Really! Probably never got over the loss of her son," pondered Della. "He wasn't very old, two or three at most. Adrian turned up to babysit one day and Florence sent him away saying the child had disappeared. For a long time people thought she'd done away with him."

"I doubt that's the answer, though it has been known," remarked Meg. "I should have asked his birthday, he'd be much easier to trace if I had that information."

Della played with her fingers whilst muttering under her breath, "Well Adrian was born February 1973, he'd only be nine or ten when he was asked to watch the child, so that would be about... 1979 or 80 and his birthday was the same day as Granny's, April 23rd."

"That's great, Della, well remembered, thank you."

"Why you looking at this anyway? Is it anything to do with Tyla?"

Meg stopped typing and turned towards her friend. "There's something I need to tell you about Tyla but I don't want you to think of this as negative."

Della's eyes teared up. "Just tell me, Meg, whatever it is," she begged.

Meg threw a glance towards Joel who appeared to have fallen asleep and lowered her tone. "We've found Tyla's toy giraffe."

"Found it, where?"

Meg took Della's hand.

"The day DS Tully was killed we were following the Cassidys to Cwmdovey. We returned a couple of days later and found an old farmhouse, that's where Tyla's giraffe was found," she explained.

"Are the Cassidys involved?"

"We think so. It appears they were using the farmhouse to hold children."

"Hold children? What does that mean, Meg, hold them for what?" cried Della.

"That, we don't know, but we're making progress. The Cassidys are mixed up in this one way or another, it's just a matter of time before we find her," soothed Meg.

"What if she doesn't have time, Meg? What if time is running out for her? I may never see my baby girl again," Della sobbed.

Joel was awake now. How much of the conversation he had absorbed was unknown, but he cradled his distraught mother without question.

Della retired early, the aftermath of Meg's revelation weighing heavy on her mind. She hadn't managed to eat, but with the aid of medication she would sleep.

***

Elliot was still in his office when Meg arrived; the room was brightly lit and the blinds open.

She ventured towards the office noticing as she approached that he was engaged in conversation. The glass was clear and Elliot's eyes lit brightly as she entered his sanctuary. His guest, however, was much less excited at her presence. Sitting on the couch was Alex McGurn fidgeting uncomfortably when he recognised Meg's face.

"Meg, what a lovely surprise," greeted Elliot, taking her coat and offering her a comfortable seat.

"This is Alex—"

"McGurn," finished Meg.

"You know each other?"

"We do, yes, Alex was just finishing police academy when I joined his father's team at the Met."

"You mean he's a policeman," joked Elliot, laughing at his ill-timed attempt at humour.

Alex rose. "Good to see you, Meg," he postured, heading for the door. "I'll be in touch, Elliot."

"Well that was a little awkward," declared Elliot.

"Awkward for him, yes," replied Meg.

"Have you eaten?" queried Elliot, changing the subject. "Fancy a tipple at the Oak Room?"

"Maybe later. I need your help with something."

"Of course, what can I do?

"Do you keep archives from the 70s and 80s?"

Elliot paused for a moment before replying, "Yes, I'm sure we do, why?"

"I'm looking for something from around that time, mind pointing me in the right direction?"

Elliot took her hand. "Come with me to my underground dungeon I call, 'the archives'," he mused.

Deep beneath the offices in a dank and dimly lit room, Elliot introduced Meg to the thousands of clippings stored within.

"Oh my god, I'll be here all night," she professed.

"Certainly not," denied Elliot. "We haven't just randomly filed things any old how, we have a proper system Meg, it's not the dark ages."

She giggled.

Elliot retrieved a couple of boxes each marked with the significant date. "If there's nothing in here we will have to revert to the microfiche," he stated.

"You take 79 and I'll take 80, but what exactly am I looking for?"

"Anything to do with a missing child aged around three, a boy called Marcus Darby. He lived on Pollard Avenue," Meg informed.

They set to work trawling through the dust-covered boxes.

"What was Alex doing here?" questioned Meg casually.

Elliot stopped briefly and looked at her. "Better not to ask, Meg," he suggested.

An hour or so later, Meg stumbled upon it, dated 30th May 1979, 'LOCAL BOY MISSING'.

The title seemed too meagre for the seriousness of the event, though the child's photograph filled most of the page. It was the same one that hung at the foot of Florence Darby's staircase.

"Got it," Meg declared, crossing the room to capture the light of a naked bulb. "Marcus Darby disappeared from outside his home on Wednesday 30th May. His mother Florence had pushed him into the garden to sleep, but when she returned to check on the boy, his pushchair was empty. Marcus is the second child to go missing in the last six months. A search of the area has to date yielded no result. If you recognise the photograph or have any information about the child's whereabouts please contact the local constabulary."

"I take it he was never found?" questioned Elliot.

"It doesn't seem so from what Florence said, but I need to check this out further. Mind if I borrow these?"

Elliot moved in close, seizing the opportunity, wrapping his arms around Meg and kissing her passionately. Meg was moved by the experience; the warmth of his embrace and the taste of his lips were intoxicating, but Fin was there too, in her head, watching.

"I'm sorry, Elliot," she muttered, pushing him away. "I can't do this right now."

Elliot was bemused. "Have I done something wrong?"

"No, nothing. It's not you, it's me. I need to figure things out. It's not fair on you to be given a false impression. The fact is, my husband turned up at the station this morning."

"I see," replied Elliot quietly.

"I've got to make a decision and I can't do that while I'm seeing you and working with him. I'm just asking for a little time, that's all."

Elliot backed away, fighting disappointment with dignity.

"Of course. Whatever you need, Meg."

She left the building wrestling tears of frustration.

"Meg."

Her name echoed, as if called by two different people at the same time.

She turned behind to see Elliot standing in the foyer of the newspaper office and in front of her, Fin, shocked at the realisation that his voice was not the only one calling his wife's name.

She didn't stop, but quickened her pace and hurried out of sight.

CHAPTER 23

He had left early that morning. No doubt resentful at the temporary suppression of his blood sport. He'd asked him to contact the police station if he hadn't already, by way of a note on the coffee table. His comings and goings were obscure, he hadn't seen him properly for days.

Rocky was wincing for breakfast. The cupboards were almost empty and porridge was the only option, but he lapped it up excitedly nonetheless. Marjorie would visit today, he'd ask her to pop to the supermarket. Marjorie was a godsend. He couldn't survive without her, especially with him behaving so childishly.

***

When Meg arrived at the police station, Alex McGurn was waiting in the lobby. He pulled her forcibly to one side as she entered, gripping her arm tightly, and didn't let go.

"Alex, let go of me," scolded Meg, but he persisted.

"Listen, we've both got something to lose. You mention anything to my father about seeing me last night and I'll go straight to that husband of yours and tell him you're messing around with Elliot Rockwell."

"Too late," smiled Meg. "He already knows."

Alex backed off slightly. "You're only here for a short time. This is my patch. If you do anything to upset that there will be consequences."

"Are you threatening me, Alex?"

"Call it a friendly warning," sniffed Alex.

Meg shook her head. "Your father would be so ashamed of you," she stated.

Alex lifted a hand towards Meg's face, but footsteps on the stairs halted it in midair.

Meg pulled away and headed toward the safety of familiar voices, leaving Alex to stare after her.

She could inform the DCI, though at the moment he had more than enough to contend with and Meg knew the revelation would do nothing more than destroy him. What would she achieve by telling him? A heartbroken middle-aged man soon to retire with an unblemished, exemplary record. Sadly, he wouldn't be remembered for that, though, it would be the disgraced son of the last DCI that would haunt Aberbarry Police Station. She would not allow Alex to ruin his father's reputation. DCI McGurn would leave in a blaze of glory, and Alex would have to live with the guilt of his betrayal. Meg would keep his secret, not for his sake, but for his father's.

***

Fin had already hit the road with Briggs. The number plate of the silver Mercedes belonging to Reuben Cassidy had been picked up on CCTV at a garage not far from the farmhouse and they'd gone to review the footage.

***

Meg headed towards Primrose Swann and placed the newspaper clipping on her desk with a shaky hand.

"Can you get me anything on this child, please, date of birth 23rd April 1979. His birth should be registered. Get me what you can, please."

"You okay? You're trembling," observed Swann.

Meg nodded. "Missed breakfast, low blood sugar." She smiled.

"Don't take your coat off, Meg, we've one last call to make on Pollard Avenue," instructed Patrick.

Celia Tucker's district nurse answered the door and led them to her bedroom.

"You've got visitors, sweetheart," she informed with a jovial tone. "They've come at just the right time, I've popped the kettle on."

Meg wanted to groan at the thought of more tea, but she smiled politely instead.

Celia was surrounded by pillows propping her fragile body in an upward position on a comfortable chair beside the window.

"What a great view you have from here," commented Meg, opening the conversation on a positive note.

Celia nodded her agreement.

"Celia's speech is, to put it politely, almost non-existent," explained the nurse, whose lanyard identified her as Dorothy Foley. "She tries, and we're hopeful, aren't we sweetheart?" she stated, bending over Celia with a magnificent smile.

"That's okay, we can ask yes-or-no questions, can't we Celia?" queried Meg.

Celia nodded again.

"We're in the neighbourhood because of the murder of Mr and Mrs Piper and then Sable Caine, who both live a couple of doors away from you."

Celia understood.

"Did you know the Pipers at all?"

Celia nodded.

"Both of them?"

This time Celia shook her head and attempted to point a finger towards herself.

"She means she knew Mrs Piper, Eva. They were friends, she visited regularly," informed Dorothy.

"Do you know of anyone who would want to hurt Eva or her husband?"

Celia nodded positively.

Meg searched her handbag.

"What do you need?" enquired Dorothy.

"Something I could use to write the alphabet on," explained Meg.

Dorothy scanned the room. "There should be a letter board here somewhere." She disappeared under the bed and emerged with the perfect piece of equipment. "I don't know why Marjorie hides it under the bed," she declared, handing it to Meg.

Celia Tucker knew.

***

Back at the station Fin and Briggs had arrived with footage of Gerald Cassidy driving the silver car on the day DS Tully was shot. Clear images of him, Reuben and Joel put them as far from the races as they could be. Besides, Ewan Davis had discovered that there were no races running in the area that day.

"He lied," stated Fin.

"I didn't expect anything else," replied Briggs. "Let's get this to the DCI."

"Granted it's evidence," began McGurn, "but we're going to need a lot more to put Gerald away for murder. Let's put a bit of pressure on though, bring in the grandson for questioning."

***

The phone rang on Constable Davis's desk.

The voice belonged to a well-spoken gentleman, who identified himself as Victor Stanmore.

Davis asked the standard questions. The answers were acceptable and he bid the caller good day.

Victor Stanmore's name was crossed off the list of neighbours who hadn't been contactable.

The list was now complete and he filed it away.

***

"Okay, Celia, let's give this a whirl," suggested Meg. "Now, the question was, do you know of anyone who would want to hurt Eva Piper or her husband?"

Progress was slow as Meg pointed to each letter and waited for Celia to indicate whether it was significant or not. Patrick wrote the letters down to form words.

"THEIR SON," was the first answer.

Meg glanced at Patrick and then Dorothy, who shook her head.

"I wasn't aware that the Pipers had a son," continued Dorothy.

Celia nodded.

"Okay, can you give me the son's name? Does it begin with the letter M?" queried Meg, remembering the initial on the baby's rattle she had found in the basement of the Pipers' house, but Celia shook her head with a definite 'no'.

"Okay, back to the board, Celia. Give me the first letter?" Meg pointed to every letter on the board, but Celia gave no indication.

"I think she's getting tired," commented the nurse. "This is the most activity Celia has experienced in the last twelve months."

Celia closed her eyes. Not because she felt sleepy; she was frustrated and Meg could sense it.

"I think we should give her another shot, Patrick, come back in a couple of days."

Patrick reluctantly agreed.

Celia heard them leave. Call themselves detectives, neither of them had noticed the trembling fingers she held signifying the letter 'V'.

Too busy checking the letter board to realise Celia was communicating by another means.

She sank into the pillows wearily and cried at her ineffectiveness in life.

***

The station car park was almost inaccessible. Gerald Cassidy and his band of brothers had parked numerous vehicles awkwardly across the whole area. Nothing was getting in or out easily.

"What the hell's going on?" questioned Patrick, squeezing through a narrow space to park his car.

Joel Cassidy and his mother Della were in the station. Joel had been brought in for questioning and the Cassidys didn't like it.

McGurn was pacing like a caged gorilla; he'd sent Briggs and Fin to the interview room.

"We can't keep him though, sir," protested Patrick, worried by the mob of angry travellers he had just witnessed.

"Don't you think I bloody well know that, Grayson?" scolded the DCI, "We're using his sister as the bait. Hopefully the mother will force answers out of him if she thinks he had anything to do with the disappearance of her daughter."

Poor Della, thought Meg. *As if she hadn't enough to contend with already.*

Constable Swann caught Meg's eye and beckoned her over.

"I've nothing for a Marcus Darby on the birth register, perhaps he was never registered," she declared.

Swann could be right. Florence Darby was unmarried and the circumstances of her pregnancy were not known. Registering the birth of her baby was admitting she'd had sex before marriage and that usually meant the child was put up for adoption. Perhaps, no one but Florence knew about the child for that reason.

"Are there any Marcuses at all in that time frame? quizzed Meg.

"I don't recall there being, but I'll double check," replied Swann.

***

Interview room 2 was the scene of nervous tension, as Joel Cassidy sat nibbling his fingernails with a face the colour of a ripe tomato and the sudden urge to urinate.

"What's this about?" scowled Della. "Can I speak to Meg Castleton?"

"All in good time, Ms Warren, you've got the next best thing, this is her husband." Briggs introduced Fin.

"Now Joel," began Fin, "you're not in any trouble, I just need to ask you a few questions, okay?"

Joel continued nibbling his fingers and said nothing.

Fin produced an image of the teen in the back seat of Gerald Cassidy's car with Reuben sitting beside him in the passenger seat.

Della stared. "When's this?" she growled at her son. "You best not have been bunking off school again."

Joel said nothing but his cheeks grew redder.

"This was taken last Tuesday," stated Fin, pointing to the date stamp in the corner of the image.

"Why weren't you in school?" Della's voice began to rise. "Well? Answer me, Joel."

Joel stropped in his chair. "I was helping Dad and Papa with something."

"What were you helping them with?" interrupted Fin.

"Just stuff," shrugged Joel.

"What kind of stuff?" demanded his mother.

"Was it stuff to do with the children at the farm?" continued the DS.

Briggs produced the photograph of a cuddly giraffe wearing a red bow tie.

Della cried out at the sight of it, her distress palpable.

Joel was beginning to weaken under the pressure of his mother's suffering.

"What do you know about your sister's disappearance, Joel?"

"Nothing."

"Did you help someone abduct her?"

"No."

"Did you help your father? Where is she, Joel? Is she being trafficked, sold on?"

Each question grew in intensity as Fin's voice demanded answers and Della's anguish increased.

Joel was afflicted, torn between the torment on his mother's face and the repercussions of snitching on the Cassidys.

The teen was distraught, battling the demons of his conscience. "Stop!" he bellowed, holding his head in his hands.

Della resumed maternal instinct and hugged her son close. "Joel, if you know something, for God's sake, tell them," she pleaded.

He strolled down the high street, through the park and down towards the primary school. He liked it there, standing, watching, scanning the playground for a future victim. He was the perpetual kid in a candy shop agonising over what to choose; there were so many tasty choices. His eyes rested upon the figure of a small girl, skipping alone on the far side of the designated play area. He approached the railings and caught her attention, supplying a conveyor of sweeties from his pocket, a bribe in exchange for her friendship.

The bell sounded and she ran excitedly towards it, turning back with a smile and a wave before disappearing inside.

This isn't 'goodbye', he thought. *This is 'see you again very soon'.*

CHAPTER 24

Three hours of interviewing with barely a break between questions. Della and Joel were exhausted, but Fin and Briggs were relentless.

Outside, the mob of angry travellers had increased in number and McGurn feared for the safety of his colleagues as they struggled to keep control. The main doors to the station were locked, but glass and metal would be no match for shotguns and pickaxes if the crowd wanted entry.

Gerald Cassidy's intense interest in his grandson's detention could only mean one thing – he feared what the boy would say. His whole future depended on Joel keeping his mouth shut.

Meg observed from the shadow of a two-way window. Della was on the verge of a breakdown and Joel appeared traumatised; the pool of urine beneath his chair confirmed it.

"Shouldn't we allow them a break, sir?" questioned Meg.

McGurn scratched his head with irritated fervour. He wanted to keep the pressure on, but Meg was right, they had nothing to hold the boy, he was free to leave at any time. Perhaps a change of tactic was called for.

"Get them some refreshments, Quinn, and take over the interview," he growled.

"I'm merely assisting, sir, I don't think I'm the right person to—" pleaded Meg, but McGurn interrupted.

"Then assist me by taking over the interview," he bawled, his cheeks swelling with anger.

Meg left the room and fed the vending machine until it supplied a mixture of sugary delicacies. Laden with treasure she re-entered and dismissed Fin and Briggs by order of McGurn.

"Meg, thank God," sighed Della with an expression of relief.

"I thought you could use these," Meg began, allowing the stash of snacks to litter the table.

Joel viewed them through swollen, red eyes before grabbing a chocolate bar and devouring it.

"When can we go home?" pleaded Della, gulping down the bottled water in desperation.

"The sooner Joel starts talking the sooner you can go," replied Meg, a hint of guilt clinging to the words as she spoke. She wanted to free her friend from the hostile situation, but the life of Tyla depended on the teenager's cooperation.

"Look, Joel, my advice is to tell the truth. You will only get caught out later if you don't and then the consequences will be far harsher."

Joel's eyes swelled with tears as he dropped the second chocolate bar, half eaten, onto the table. "It's not that easy," he blubbed.

"Yes it is," soothed Della, taking her son's hand in hers. "I promise you, Joel, everything will be okay as long as you tell the truth."

Joel collapsed into his mother's arms, burying his head deep into her chest as the tears flowed uncontrollably.

Meg waited for the storm to calm. Joel was on the verge of unburdening himself. She nodded agreeably to Della, signalling that she was doing the right thing.

Meg retrieved a photograph of Tyla and placed it on the table.

"Look at your sister, Joel, she needs her big brother to save her, she needs you to tell the truth."

Joel sobbed between words. "I never meant to hurt her."

She was sitting on the steps of the primary school, waiting, no parent in sight. The playground was empty; she'd been abandoned yet again.

He hurried forward knowing that at any minute a teacher would emerge and usher her back inside.

He approached with a smile and the offer of sweeties. Two were enough to bribe her into taking his hand. He'd accompany her safely home, at her mother's request.

She chatted and skipped beside him. To the outside world he was the caring grandparent. Inside he was a barren empath, motivated by the powerful urge to exert dominance over the innocence of childhood.

She climbed into the car without a second thought. He smiled; how easy it was to extract her from society, how accomplished was his ability to gain her trust.

***

"Okay, Joel, let's start at the beginning, the night of Tyla's disappearance. Tell me what happened," began Meg softly.

"I let Dad into the house and he took her from her bed, then I locked the door and went back to my room."

"Okay, so your dad, being Reuben Cassidy, came into your house during the night, removed your sister from her bed and left?" she reiterated.

"Yes."

Della was struggling to control her emotions. One wrong word could jeopardise the interview and as much as Meg sympathised, she couldn't risk Joel clamming up now. She reached for Della's hand and squeezed it reassuringly.

"You're doing great, Joel," Meg soothed. "Now where did your dad take Tyla, do you know?"

"To a farmhouse."

"Do you know where that farmhouse is?" continued Meg, conscious that the dwelling in question had already been discovered.

"I've been there, but I couldn't find it again."

"How many times have you been there?"

"Just once, we were supposed to..." Joel stopped mid-sentence, suddenly fearful of the information he was about to divulge.

Meg studied him closely, the dark fringe of curls that framed his face, the fear in his tear-filled eyes, the quiver in his youthful voice. He wasn't a man, nor was he a boy, he had entered the difficult phase of metamorphosis. Furthermore he was a Cassidy and that was probably the most arduous burden any teen could endure.

"You were going to the farmhouse on that Tuesday the police officer was shot and killed?"

Joel lowered his head, not daring to make eye contact, but nodded in agreement.

"Oh my god, Joel!" cried Della. "What's going to be next, robbing old ladies at knifepoint?"

"Della, please, you can have your say when I'm finished asking questions," Meg scolded. "This is you, Joel, in the back of your father's car," she stated, producing the image caught on CCTV.

Joel nodded.

Meg glanced towards the darkened pane of glass that divided the interview room from its clandestine neighbour.

McGurn had been waiting for a signal. Joel had given them enough to bring Reuben and Gerald Cassidy in for questioning, but that would be easier said than done amidst their cult of followers.

"So your dad took Tyla to the farmhouse, and then what happens?" continued Meg, eager to extract as much information as possible.

"Dad said she'd be safe there."

"Safe... safe from who?"

Joel tentatively glanced towards Della who gasped with shock.

"From your mother?" queried Meg.

"Dad said you couldn't be trusted to look after her. Said she was a Cassidy and should live with the Cassidys."

"And why can't I be trusted?" demanded Della.

"You were going to sell Tyla to the Pipers to get money for drugs."

This was not how Meg had imagined the conversation going, but she pressed forward ignoring Della's cries of desperation.

"Did your dad explain why Tyla would be sold to the Pipers?"

"He said they had a racquet going in stolen children, sold them on to people who couldn't have any of their own."

Joel's explanation gave clarity to his behaviour. Joel thought he was doing the best thing for Tyla by allowing his father to remove her from the family home.

"Where is Tyla now?" came the final and most relevant question.

"Dad said somewhere safe, but I don't know where that is, and that's the truth."

CHAPTER 25

McGurn emerged from the station, a posse of officers around him. He raised a calming hand as the roar of abuse flowed across the car park in a wave of hostility.

"Joel is on his way home, I suggest you do the same," he bellowed.

Gerald gave the signal and the throng began to disperse.

McGurn waited until the crowd had abated sufficiently, before ordering his constables to detain Reuben and Gerald Cassidy.

He'd gone for a stroll under the cover of darkness. The child was settled for the night; chloroform had seen to that.

He paced the length of the avenue and back again. It was quiet now; the bustle of police activity and flow of vehicles had slowed. Getting rid of the gossiping female slut had thrown his neighbourhood into the spotlight, a consequence of his impulsive action. He'd had to curb his appetite as a result, but order had resumed and he was free to 'scratch his ever-growing itch'.

The light of a first-floor window blinked, catching his attention. The faint outline of a person moved in its shadow, someone sitting beside the window watching him.

He hadn't noticed it before, he was always too lost in his own thoughts and distractions. The window had a direct line of sight to the Pipers' house and for that matter, most of one side of the avenue. He pondered about who lived there. Perhaps he ought to pay them a visit.

***

When Meg arrived at Della's later that evening, Fin was waiting.

Joel had gone directly to bed, exhausted and embarrassed. Della had hit the wine hard and lay comatose on the living room sofa.

"I've ordered Chinese food," announced Fin as Meg entered the room. "Thought you'd be too tired to cook."

"Della usually cooks," she answered curtly.

"Well no chance of that tonight," mused Fin.

Meg cast aside her coat and shoes, collapsing on to the kitchen sofa.

"Honestly, Fin, I just wanted a hot bath and an early night," she informed, "not a Chinese banquet and the third degree."

"You still can," proffered Fin. "Let's eat then I'll leave you alone."

Meg doubted that very much but before she could answer the food order arrived.

"Why so much food?" questioned Meg, spreading the cartons of Asian cuisine across the table.

"I didn't know what you wanted, so I ordered all of your favourites," replied Fin with a smile.

Meg was hungry and the feast smelled divine.

When the foil trays were empty and not a morsel remained she returned to the comfort of the sofa.

"Fancy a cuppa, Meg?"

She nodded. Meg could feel the stress of the day draining away and sleep was stalking her.

"Sorry about the other night," confessed Fin. "I hadn't realised you'd been visiting the newspaper office."

Meg recognised the signs of Fin's well-established interview technique. He was about to unleash a barrage of questions, unmistakably the true reason for his visit.

"Let me stop you there, Fin," she answered abruptly. "Elliot Rockwell and I are friends and that's all I'm going to say about it."

"Just friends?"

"Yes, just friends."

"That's not the story in the men's locker room." The sentence fired from his lips like a ballistic missile.

"I don't care what the story is in the men's locker room. No doubt spoken by the slanderous Alex McGurn. I'm telling you we're just friends."

Fin backed off slightly, navigating his way through Della's congested cupboards in search of tea cups.

"Okay, if you say so. No need to get defensive."

Meg knew Fin's tactics all too well, the hint of sarcasm in his voice and the aloofness to his tone desperately masking the curiosity that was screaming for answers inside him. She wasn't going to play his game. He hadn't cared to contact her even to discuss his arrival as the new DS. She would leave him to stew in his own insecurities.

"I'm going for that bath now, I'll see you at work tomorrow."

***

Reuben and Gerald Cassidy had spent a night in the cells. Their aggressive detention had afforded them both the necessary time to cool off.

Reuben was taken to the interview room, where DI Grayson and DS Castleton waited. His arrogant demeanour was unsettling and the defiant smirk that crossed his lips indicative of his confidence.

Gregory DuPlessis followed him into the room. The lawyer was a long-time associate of the Cassidys, no doubt knee deep in corruption himself, though that would be almost impossible to prove.

DuPlessis was an elegant man, undeniably handsome with the debonair charm of aristocracy. He filled the station with the intoxicating scent of French cologne. He wore a signature cravat locked in position by a handmade shirt from Savile Row and crocodile skin brogues, which matched his expensive leather briefcase.

He could not have been further removed from his notorious client, who sat unshaven, shoddily dressed and sporting the distinct odour of stale sweat.

Nevertheless, he greeted him with a hearty handshake and familial small talk.

"Let's begin, shall we?" declared Patrick, opening the buff folder in front of him.

He placed the photograph of Tyla Cassidy on the table and pushed it in Reuben's direction.

"Recognise her?" questioned Patrick.

"Course I do," scoffed Reuben. "Is that a trick question?"

"Where is she?" Patrick was straight to the point.

The traveller folded his arms and yawned disrespectfully. He tossed a glance at DuPlessis who nodded agreeably.

"Where is she, Reuben? You're not doing yourself any favours by withholding evidence. If you tell us where she is we might be able to help reduce your sentence."

DuPlessis struck like a defensive viper. "Are you bribing my client for information, Inspector?"

"Not at all, sir, I'm merely suggesting it would be in your client's best interests to help us with our enquiries."

The two men locked eyes, like hormone-fuelled beasts fighting for their masculinity.

Castleton sensed the tension and intervened. "We know you took Tyla Cassidy from her home in the middle of the night. We know you kept her at the farmhouse near Cwmdovey. What we need to know from you is where she is now."

"No comment," declared Reuben.

Castleton pressed on. "We know you were in the car with your father and son on the day DS Tully was shot and killed. We know it was you or your father that murdered him. We know you weren't at the races, Reuben, so stop being such a dick and tell us where the child is."

Reuben snorted and cleared his throat of the offensive phlegm that lodged there. He coughed and spat it out.

DuPlessis remained unperturbed by the disgusting behaviour.

"He must be on a good number to sit and defend that animal," scowled McGurn, watching the interview from the shadow of the two-way mirror.

"Got a fag?" demanded Reuben.

"Depends," answered Castleton.

"On what?"

"On what you tell us."

"Look, the kid's all right. It was a practical joke on that sorry excuse of a mother. Was gonna bring her back eventually," grinned Reuben.

"In that case you could have told us that in the beginning. Saved us thousands on a widespread manhunt. Divers, sniffer dogs, you getting the picture, Mr Cassidy? Withholding evidence, perverting the course of justice, abduction, not to mention the possibility of murder. It's going to be a heavy sentence and 'no comment' is not going to cut it."

Fin was at his best now, forceful and direct, unaffected by the traveller's intimidating gestures and above all, he was pragmatic.

"I can't be done for taking my own child," grunted Reuben.

"But she's not your child, is she Mr Cassidy?"

"She's got my name," he declared as though the girl's surname endorsed his actions.

DuPlessis rolled his eyes and leaned close to whisper.

Reuben fidgeted on hearing the lawyer's words. He stared questioningly as DuPlessis nodded affirmatively.

"I don't know where she is, but she's safe."

"And the others?" queried Castleton.

DuPlessis appeared bemused and looked to Reuben for an explanation.

"They're all okay. Pa took 'em somewhere safe. I only took Tyla, I swear, and I never shot the cop neither."

Reuben Cassidy had unwittingly sealed the fate of his father, Gerald.

Reuben was directed back to the cells. It was for the CPS to decide his fate, that is, if he managed to stay alive after Gerald discovered that he had squealed.

***

That afternoon Meg felt the need leave the station for a while. The air was thick with testosterone and they were no closer to knowing the whereabouts of Tyla Cassidy or her fate.

Reuben was remanded in custody and would appear before magistrates the following day. Gerald was yet to be interviewed. McGurn had obtained a further twenty-four hours and decided that dealing with one Cassidy was enough for that day.

Meg headed to Della's to check on her; she hadn't seen her since she left the station with Joel the day before.

Della was crashed out – an empty bottle of vodka had been her companion. Joel had hopefully gone to school. His bedroom was empty and his school bag missing.

Elliot had been texting since Meg had rejected him a couple of nights earlier. She wanted to reply but what would she say? The fact is, she's married and wasn't consciously looking for a replacement when Elliot appeared on the scene.

She turned off her phone and pushed the thoughts of men to the back of her mind.

She crossed the road towards Celia Tucker's house; a car was reversing from its driveway and drove slowly past. The driver wore a flat cap and overcoat. His face seemed familiar. Meg looked back to where the car had emerged. It was the blind man's house, the driver must have been his brother.

Celia Tucker was sleeping when Meg entered her bedroom. She was nothing more than a skeleton in patterned pyjamas, Meg thought to herself, noticing the bony protrusions that poked from her brushed cotton nightwear, and the scrawny ankles that dangled beneath the weight of fur-trimmed slippers. Her cheeks were hollow, chiselled by the depression of loose skin, and she wore a sallow shade of renal failure.

Her bedroom, her prison, was lacking the luxuries of a female boudoir, replaced by the necessities of her requirements. Catheter bags and oxygen tanks, an army of pill bottles and emollients, sippy cups, some empty, some half full, adult bibs and enough boxes of rubber gloves to sink a ship.

Celia stirred involuntarily, the shock of muscular spasm jolting her into consciousness. She smiled crookedly, delighted by Meg's presence. Meg fluffed the pillows around her and offered the sippy cup half filled with orange juice. Celia drank enthusiastically, unaware of the constant dribble that seeped from one corner of her mouth. Meg wiped away the liquid remnants and perched herself on the bed.

"I thought I'd come back to see you," she began. "I felt like we had unfinished business."

Celia nodded.

"You were tired and a bit frustrated, but if you're feeling up to it we can try the letter board?"

Celia nodded again.

Meg searched the room for the helpful object but it was nowhere to be found, not even under the bed where Dorothy, the district nurse, had said it was usually kept.

Celia looked downhearted at its disappearance.

"Not to worry," soothed Meg, "I have some paper and a pen in my bag, we will make our own."

Meg laid out the alphabet on A4 paper just as it appeared on the missing letter board.

"Okay, Celia, I think we're ready to rock and roll." She chuckled as a hint of sparkle danced in the woman's eyes.

"You told me that you knew of someone who might want to hurt the Pipers, is that correct?"

Celia nodded.

"We were going to spell out the name of that person, but Dorothy said you were too tired to continue. I felt that you were frustrated because you don't actually know the person's name, am I correct?"

Celia nodded as vigorously as her paralysed movement would allow.

"I thought so." Meg smiled at her intuitiveness. "Is the person someone the Pipers knew?"

Again Celia nodded.

"A family member?"

Celia shook her head.

"A friend perhaps?"

Celia shook again. This time she raised a trembling finger and pointed out into the street.

Meg thought for a moment, then asked, "A neighbour?"

Celia nodded triumphantly.

"We're making great progress, Celia, well done," Meg praised, offering the sippy cup for a second time.

Meg turned over the sheet of paper wearing the alphabet and drew an outline of Pollard Avenue. She labelled Della's house, the Pipers', Florence Darby's, Sable Caine's, the blind man's and Celia's.

She placed the drawing on Celia's lap and pointed to each house in turn. Celia shook her head until Meg came to the blind man's house, then she nodded desperately.

Meg retrieved the paper and marked the house with an X.

"You do know that the man who lives there is blind, don't you?" she queried.

Celia nodded positively.

"Then it would be very difficult for a blind man to have killed the Pipers," she explained, but Celia threw her head from side to side aggressively, suggesting she disagreed.

"The blind man has a brother, could it be him?"

Celia shook her head.

The conversation was becoming fruitless. Celia Tucker was obviously muddled; first she indicated that a blind man could have harmed the Pipers and then she denied that he had a brother, who Meg had just witnessed on the way to visit Celia.

Meg felt slightly awkward as she checked her watch. "I'm sorry, Celia, we will have to leave it there for now, I have a meeting to get to. Perhaps I can visit again."

Celia tried desperately to force out words, but only produced a series of undecipherable sounds.

Meg left under a cloud of guilt. Celia obviously had something to say, but it seemed impossible to find out what.

Celia cradled the two fingers she had so desperately wanted the young detective to notice. She hadn't bothered to ask Celia about the last few letters of the alphabet, distracted by details of the blind man and his brother. Celia despaired. Her imprisoned voice would never be able to communicate her belief. The situation, like her life, was hopeless.

CHAPTER 26

Gerald Cassidy was a force of nature that no one seemed keen to interview. In the end McGurn nominated DS Castleton and DI Grayson to take the first shift.

"We need a confession," the DCI instilled. "I've got a search warrant in transit and it would be fantastic if we could lay our hands on the weapon, but a confession would definitely nail the bastard."

Grayson and Castleton exchanged glances. It was highly unlikely that Gerald Cassidy would confess to anything let alone the murder of a police sergeant.

"What about the girl?" probed Castleton. "Shall we ask him about that first?"

"Obviously the child's our priority and he'll do time for that, but you and I both know that murder is a whole different ball game. Just get a confession to something, that'll be a start," advised the DCI.

Gerald sat smugly beside his barrister, Nathaniel DuPlessis, the brother of Gregory. Nathaniel was a shorter, plumper version; his hair was thinning and he hadn't been blessed with the same good looks, but his reputation was legendary. He appeared shoddy and unshaven, surprising for someone taking home a six-figure salary. In fact, at first glance it was difficult to ascertain which of the two men was the client.

"Right, let's get started, shall we?" began Castleton, retrieving a photograph of Tyla Cassidy from his file. He placed it on the table and stabbed it with a finger. "Where is she, Gerald?"

Gerald cast a sideways glance to his barrister. "No introductions, Officer, no 'sorry to have kept you waiting, Mr Cassidy', no refreshments." He tutted. "Not very polite, is it, Nate?"

The lawyer managed a slight smile.

"Perhaps it would be prudent to offer my client some refreshments, Officers, in view of his overnight detention," suggested the lawyer with pompous elocution.

Patrick ordered coffee and toast for the distasteful traveller, who ate noisily and slowly while the officers looked on impatiently.

"Okay, Mr Cassidy," snapped Castleton the moment the last mouthful of toast disappeared into the suspect's mouth. "I ask you again, where is she?"

Gerald withdrew a pair of reading glasses from his back pocket and strained over the photograph as if he were seeing the little girl's face for the very first time.

"Pretty little thing, ain't she?" he scoffed. "Never seen her before in my life."

"Really! That's strange. She's a Cassidy like you, your grandson's sister. I find it hard to believe that you've never seen her before."

"Believe what you like," growled Gerald, folding his glasses.

"You see, Gerald, a few hours ago your son, Reuben, told us that he abducted the girl from her bed and took her to a farmhouse near Cwmdovey. He says you know where she is and it was you who shot DS Tully."

Gerald, though physically unperturbed by the statement was mentally wrestling to believe that his own son would have said such a thing. His pupils dilated and briefly he was lost for words.

"I don't believe you, you're just trying it on." He smirked, but behind the jovial façade Gerald was battling with uncertainty.

"We know that Tyla Cassidy was kept at the farmhouse along with nine other children. The place is littered with their DNA."

Gerald said nothing.

"We know the house belongs to the Pipers' son, Marcus."

Gerald's face creased with a blank expression. "Who the bloody hell's Marcus?" he quipped.

Castleton persisted. "You killed the Pipers, abducted the children, sold them on and kept the profit for yourself. You're looking at three counts of murder, Gerald, and ten of abduction. You'll be lucky to see the outside world again."

Gerald was simmering now, anger and uncertainty bubbling inside. Castleton was sure an eruption was imminent as he pressed on.

"Granted Reuben will probably serve a bit of time, we made a deal with him, minimal jail time for maximum confession."

That was the moment Gerald Cassidy exploded. He threw his chair across the room and launched himself over the table, grabbing Castleton by the neck. Grayson pressed the alarm, officers stormed the room and prised the traveller from DS Castleton's throat.

"I'm okay," spluttered Castleton, "but put him in cuffs."

Gerald, hands safely locked behind his back, resumed his seat.

"Well, Gerald, anything you want to tell us?" questioned Grayson, taking over whilst his colleague regained composure.

Gerald threw a questioning glance to his barrister, a perceptive nod back supplying the answer.

"Well?" demanded Grayson.

"The kid was Reuben's idea. He wanted to upset the mother. He brought her to the site, but she wouldn't stop howling and crying, so I suggested he take her up to the farmhouse out of the way. The other kids up there were waiting to be picked up. Somehow she got mixed up with them and was taken as well. She wasn't supposed to, Reuben was going to take her home the next day, but when we got up there all ten of 'em was gone."

"And where were the other kids being taken to?"

"Well that was down to the Pipers. All I did was deliver the kids, they took care of the rest. When they turned up dead, I had no idea what happened to the children."

Gerald's answer seemed plausible but with many discrepancies.

"So you worked with the Pipers?"

"Not worked, more collaborated."

"And what was in it for you?"

"Money, of course."

"You abducted children for money?"

"We all have to earn a living, Officer. You do it your way, I do it mine."

"You really are a low life, aren't you, Cassidy?"

DuPlessis objected to the remark, but Patrick persisted.

"Tell me about the Pipers?"

"Not much to tell, we met once, conducted business via the farmhouse. They got in touch when they were ready for the next lot of kids."

"What do you think they were doing with the children?"

"It's obvious, isn't it? Selling 'em on."

"Selling them on for what and to whom?" Grayson's temples throbbed with disgust.

"Probably the dark web, porn, there's a lot of money in that, the nonces can't get enough of it and some are willing to pay any price," smirked Gerald.

Patrick wanted to dive across the table and beat Cassidy's selfish, money-oriented carcass black and blue. He swallowed his disdain and pushed the file towards Castleton.

"Are you done now?" grumbled Cassidy. "These cuffs are bloody uncomfortable."

"No, we're not finished, Mr Cassidy. In fact, we're just getting started."

Evening was closing in rapidly. He had a busy schedule. The girl in the basement was ready to display. He'd chosen the steps of the primary school, where he'd first set eyes on her. It was fitting that she should return there and it was a certainty that she would be found. He lifted her body from the boot of his car and positioned her carefully on the middle step. He placed her elbows on her knees and propped her head onto open hands. She looked angelic, as though she had fallen asleep whilst waiting to be picked up.

He sat and waited until he was sure the coast was clear then he drove away and headed towards home.

***

"You got a death wish, Castleton?" queried McGurn. "That stunt you pulled nearly got you killed."

"Well you wanted to get him for something, sir," Castleton mused.

"Yes, but not your bloody murder."

Finlay Castleton had lost his zest for life. His marriage was failing, his wife was being unfaithful and the traumas of Brightmarsh still haunted his nightmares. In that moment he hadn't cared if Gerald Cassidy had ended it all, he was almost willing it to happen, he had nothing left to live for.

"You want me to send Briggs in?" questioned McGurn as Cassidy was brought from his cell once again.

"Hell no!" interrupted Patrick. "He's too emotional over Tully, we'll see it through."

"Good man." The DCI patted him gratefully.

Behind the scenes officers had been feverishly working to provide substantial evidence of Cassidy's involvement. CCTV had offered the first sighting of a blue Transit van emerging from the lane to the farmhouse and heading in the direction of the docks. It was followed on most of its journey, but then disappeared before entering the docklands. The registration had been traced and an address provided. It was assumed this was the vehicle that had transported Tyla Cassidy and the other children to their next destination.

The Pipers' bank accounts had been scrutinised, showing large transactions being credited from a company called Hamelin Holdings. Payments had been transferred to Gerald Cassidy's account on a sporadic basis.

The blue van belonged to Eddie O'Shea, who resided in Dublin. DC Briggs was already on his way to Ireland.

The search of Cassidy's property had yielded no firearm matching the description of the bullet that killed DS Tully, which came as no surprise to anyone. Cassidy was illiterate, but he wasn't stupid.

"Okay, he's back in the interview room," McGurn informed.

Grayson and Castleton entered with a renewed vigour. Cassidy and his barrister were chatting casually.

"Right then, Mr Cassidy, you've had a slight reprieve, the cuffs have been removed, so let's get down to business," began Castleton. He placed an image of the blue van on the table. "Recognise this vehicle?"

Cassidy glanced towards it. "Can't say I do, no."

"Really! Are you sure? Take another look."

Cassidy denied the request.

"How about the name Eddie O'Shea?"

A glint of recognition sparked in Gerald's eyes, but he shook his head in denial.

"What about Hamelin Holdings?"

This time he glanced towards DuPlessis who shook his head.

"It's only a matter of time before we have the whole picture, Gerald, it would be in your best interests to co-operate with us."

Again DuPlessis shook his head.

"Okay, you can go back to the cells." Castleton closed his file and rose to leave the room.

"I'm afraid you've run out of time, Officer, you can't hold my client any longer," boasted the barrister.

"I'm afraid we can, Mr DuPlessis, we've got an extension for a further forty-eight hours."

"On what charge?"

"Abduction, exploitation of children, perverting the course of justice, need I go on?"

Gerald pulled DuPlessis aside. A brief interlude of low whispers saw the barrister ask for a plea bargain on Cassidy's behalf.

"I can't promise you anything, Gerald," stated Castleton. "Besides, it depends on what you are prepared to disclose. It will, of course, be made known that you co-operated, which may or may not reduce your sentence."

Gerald took his seat.

"Eddie O'Shea runs a trafficking ring out of Ireland. He sells young children for obscene amounts of money, and that's all I know."

"When you say he sells the children, who does he sell them to?"

"The highest bidder."

"Get on to the Child Abuse Investigation Team," growled McGurn to Briggs. "Send them Tyla Cassidy's photograph and any others we have from the children who were kept at the farmhouse. I need to know whether any of them have cropped up on the dark web."

Briggs disappeared hastily.

"Bloody disgusting," uttered McGurn, "making money from the abuse of small children. They want stringing up and their balls chopping off."

Meg agreed. How could she break the news to Della that her child could have been shipped off to God knows where, having God knows what done to her? Perhaps it was best to say nothing until she had definitive confirmation.

CHAPTER 27

Celia Tucker was the first visit on Dorothy Foley's rota that morning. She let herself in as usual, retrieving the key from a security box beside the front door.

"It's only me, Celia," she announced. "I'm nice and early today."

Celia couldn't answer, but Dorothy always liked to declare her presence. She headed for the kitchen like she always did on morning visits, to make porridge and tea for her patient.

Up the stairs she headed with the tray of breakfast fare and placed it at the foot of the bed.

Celia appeared to be sleeping, but then Dorothy noticed the stain of red liquid pooled at her feet.

Celia was dead, slain like a wild animal, bathing in her own blood, gutted from sternum to pelvis.

Dorothy screamed and fumbled for her phone, trembling as she dialled for assistance.

Celia Tucker had been murdered.

***

It was a wild and blustery day as DC Briggs exited his rental car on the outskirts of Dublin, in the small rural town of Colkinney. It was a hamlet of scattered, well-proportioned properties. He stood on the driveway of one such house, the home of Eddie O'Shea. A magnificent display of windows dissected by lengths of enormous oak timber greeted him. The entrance only discernible by its dual lighting and welcome mat.

A young lady answered the door, dressed in gym clothes, her hair dangling from a neat pony tail.

"Can I help you?" she asked.

"I'm DC Briggs from Aberbarry in Wales. I'm looking for Eddie O'Shea, is he in?"

Without another word the girl disappeared and the shouts of, "Dad, there's someone at the door for you," echoed in the vastness of the hallway.

A man appeared; slim, peppered grey hair, green eyes, clad in designer track suit. "What can I do for you?" he enquired pleasantly.

Briggs flashed his identity card and the man invited him inside.

The home was an extravagant expanse of luxury, oozing opulence and labelled accessories with every turn of the head.

The young woman had disappeared, but another woman, much the same in age, was preparing food in the kitchen. A large woolly sheepdog lounged beside a roaring fire and an older woman, who Briggs deduced to be O'Shea's wife, graced one side of an extensive sofa, lost in the pages of a gossip magazine.

O'Shea led the DC to his office at the back of the house. Equally as lavish, but with a practical twist. O'Shea parked himself behind a leather-topped desk and offered Briggs a seat.

"So what's this about, Officer?" questioned O'Shea.

Briggs withdrew the image of the blue van and passed it across the desk.

"This van is registered to you, sir, is that correct?"

"Indeed it is, though I have to admit that I have never driven the thing," scoffed O'Shea, handing the image back.

"Why's that then, sir?"

O'Shea leaned forward and placed his fingertips together on the desk. "Well, if you noticed what I have sitting on my driveway, I'd say it was blatantly obvious."

Briggs recalled the expensive array of cars parked side by side at the foot of a row of garages. He couldn't imagine O'Shea tucked behind the wheel of the shabby blue van, in his valuable Rolex and designer threads.

"I see, sir, so if you don't drive it, who does?"

O'Shea hesitated. "What's this about?" he demanded.

"It's about your van being linked to a trafficking ring of small children... sir!"

O'Shea sniggered. "Don't be ridiculous. A trafficking ring?"

Eddie was convincing but Briggs detected the hint of underlying unease in his tone.

"So sir, who drives the van?"

"Any of my employees, Officer, whoever needs it on the day."

"What business are you in?"

"Scrap metal."

"Looks like you've done well out of it," commented Briggs.

"I've done all right. Now are we finished? I have business to attend to."

Briggs ignored the question and continued, "Where is the van now?"

"At the yard, I expect."

"I need you to take me there, it's to be impounded for forensics," stated Briggs.

O'Shea dithered for a moment, then grabbed a set of car keys from beneath the desk.

"Rosa, I'm going out for a bit. Keep my lunch warm, will you?" he demanded of the girl in the kitchen. She nodded and gave Briggs a solemn glance. He wondered if Rosa was the result of trafficking herself.

"Follow me," demanded O'Shea, jumping into a highly polished, black Bentley.

Briggs did as requested, stopping at a factory-style building some five miles from the Irishman's home. The place was a hive of activity with blue vans coming and going in clockwork fashion.

DC Briggs spied the registration plate of the van in question and headed towards it. A young man was busy valeting the inside, but he stopped as Briggs approached.

Briggs flashed his ID.

"Move away from the van please, sir," he ordered.

Hopefully whatever evidence was being sucked into the depths of the hoovering device had stopped soon enough to leave sufficient DNA for forensics to find.

Briggs called for a tow truck and waited until the blue van was secure and driving off in the direction of the docks.

Eddie O'Shea was watching from the window of his factory. Briggs headed inside to find him.

"I'm going to need the details of the driver for these dates, please." He handed the list to O'Shea who immediately passed it to a woman, who appeared to be his secretary.

She disappeared into an adjoining room and returned victorious with the required information.

DC Briggs bid the Irishman good day and headed for the exit. Just as he reached the top step of the staircase, he heard an office phone ring. The secretary promptly answered with a jovial, "Good morning, Hamelin Holdings."

CHAPTER 28

Meg and Patrick had arrived at the home of Celia Tucker, just in time to witness her desecrated body leaving under cover of black plastic.

Patrick stopped the gurney and unzipped. Celia bore the same hallmark as the previous murders.

To make matters worse, at the same time as Celia's body was en route to the mortuary, McGurn made contact directing them to the primary school, where the body of a child had been discovered by the caretaker.

"It's going to be one of those days," sighed Patrick.

"Isn't it always?" replied Meg.

***

At the primary school, Mr Bythesea, the caretaker who had discovered the child's body, was locked in the male bathroom dispelling the contents of his breakfast.

Eventually he appeared, ashen and trembling.

"I arrived like I always do around 6.30. I was buffing the main corridor towards the front door. I could a see figure through the glass. I thought it was a very early pupil sitting on the steps. I unlocked the entrance and came outside to see what she was doing. It was only as I stepped closer I realised she was dead." Mr Bythesea's eyes pooled with tears.

"Did you touch her?" queried Meg.

"Well when she didn't respond to my voice, her eyes were closed so I thought she was sleeping and it was so cold I wanted to wake her and take her inside. I prodded her gently, she collapsed in a heap and that's when I... Poor Maisie." He buried his head in his chest and cried.

McGurn arrived for an update and began barking orders in every direction. "I want CCTV from that camera," he demanded, pointing at the one that faced the school's entrance. "What the hell is going on? Two in one day? That's four children at my reckoning and now four adults," he protested. "We need to get a lid on this before there are any more."

***

Back at the station Constable Davis was making contact with the families of children whose DNA had been identified at the farmhouse. Primrose Swann and Katie Alder were still trawling through reams of information in the search for Marcus Darby.

Two children had been identified by sharing the same birthday with Marcus; one had emigrated to New Zealand and been eliminated whilst the other was traced to a hospital in Cwmdovey following an admission forty years earlier.

Meg contacted the hospital and asked for records to be forwarded. Within minutes an email arrived with attached discharge notes from the hospital's accident and emergency department. She browsed them quickly, searching for anything that might indicate the child and Marcus Darby were one and the same.

Their blood groups matched, not unusual since theirs was the most common, along with the majority of the population.

Then she found it. She'd almost missed it as she scrolled through the documentation, but on the page marked 'parental consent' sat the signature of Eva Piper, just below the child's name, Marcus Piper.

Meg dashed into McGurn's office triumphantly. She needed permission to access the child's DNA and match it with the Pipers'. Furthermore she needed Florence Darby to provide a sample and if what she suspected was the case, Marcus Piper was actually Florence Darby's long-lost son.

McGurn viewed the evidence.

The child had sustained fractured ribs and right arm after falling from a tree in the garden, it stated. He was a thin boy, well beneath the growth percentile for his age. He appeared pale and unkempt. The mother would not leave the boy's side but he seemed uncomfortable in her presence. The child never spoke. He was observed to demonstrate unusual habits, i.e. the eating of ice cream with his fingers, as though he had never seen or used cutlery before. The case was referred to social services querying neglect. To be reviewed in six weeks for removal of the cast.

"Is there nothing from the six-week visit?" questioned the DCI.

"No, he didn't attend for the review."

"Okay, if the hospital still holds the boy's DNA then get it tested against the Pipers'."

"What about Florence Darby, sir?"

"Let's see where we get to, Quinn, before we start giving false hope to a vulnerable old lady. In the meantime find out which school he went to and chase up social services for their information."

Meg made several calls that afternoon, all of them regarding Marcus Piper. She was passed between departments by social services until she finally reached a lady who had inherited the child's file.

"There's not much I can tell you, Detective. I visited the house on several occasions, but each time I was denied access," informed the social worker.

"So you never actually saw the child?" quizzed Meg.

"Sadly, no, the parents had the right to choose. If they said no to me entering the home, there was nothing I could do about it."

"Did you suspect any wrongdoing?"

"Not that I can remember, we are talking decades ago and I'm about ready to retire. From the little I can gain from the file, he was never followed up after the fourth visit was declined."

"So you have no idea what happened to him, or whether he was still alive?" Meg growled, annoyed at the incompetency of the social worker.

"I'm sorry to say, I didn't," admitted the voice. "The workload was overwhelming. It was easy for a child to get lost in the system," she defended.

Meg ended the call, muttering in disgust at the appalling failure that had plagued Marcus Piper's young life.

CHAPTER 29

The child had been found; it had made the headlines once more. *The infamous child pose killer strikes again*, he thought to himself. There was the clean-up in the basement to attend to, but he wasn't feeling in a cleaning mood. He counted the stairs down to the cellar and stopped, removing his treasure trove from behind the step. If this carried on much longer he'd have to get a bigger biscuit tin; the precious locks of hair that lay inside were growing so rapidly he feared they would crush and entangle.

He checked the contents of his box, each plait inducing a memory of the children he'd snipped it from, nestled securely for safekeeping within his faded Christmas tin.

He folded the plastic sheeting coated with dried blood and carried it upstairs. He hung it back above the bath and sprayed and scrubbed until every inch of sanguine remnant disappeared into the drain. The amount of shower curtains he went through was unbelievable, but it was a genius idea using them to catch the child's blood and bodily fluids.

It looked as good as new. He wouldn't need to buy another one yet, not this time anyway.

***

Eddie O'Shea's blue van had arrived for forensic testing along with DC Briggs. The fact that the vehicle and Hamelin Holdings belonged to the Irishman left a multitude of questions.

Did O'Shea know that the van was being used to traffic children? Most certainly, as payments to the Pipers' bank account came from Hamelin Holdings, his company.

Was the scrap metal business merely a front to cover the truth and launder large sums of money?

How had Eddie O'Shea made so much money?

The truth came in the form of forensic evidence. A trace of white powder had been discovered in the back of the van – cocaine. DNA matched with that of Tyla Cassidy and two other children from the farmhouse, confirming that at some point they had ridden in the back of the blue Transit. Further DNA matched a known felon named Boyd O'Leary. His prints infested the steering wheel and door handles. Obviously he hadn't reckoned on police involvement.

"Boyd O'Leary," sniggered McGurn. "A boil on the face of humanity. A devious bastard and cousin to the Cassidys He'd sell his own grandmother for a pint of Guinness. He's the devil in disguise, a wolf in sheep's clothing."

"You've obviously met before," prompted Meg.

"Oh yes, too many times, Quinn. Bring the little toe rag in for questioning."

***

Fin had kept a low profile for the last few days, ensuring that he was never in the same place as Meg at the same time. Quite an amazing feat in a police station the size of a shoe box. Elliot's text messages had ceased and Meg had thrown herself into the ongoing investigations with little time for thoughts of anything else.

Perhaps when this was all over and they returned to Brightmarsh, they could sit down and talk it through like adults, but until then Meg was happy to leave men and marriage for another day.

***

Finally, the DNA results came back. The child the Pipers had paraded as their own was in no way related to either of them. It was time to pay Florence Darby another visit.

Florence was her usual spritely self. Dressed in chequered slacks and yellow pullover, she guided Meg into the jungle and busied herself at once with refreshments.

"So lovely to see you again, dear," she smiled, whilst buttering scones with a flourish of jam and cream.

"I thought I'd just check in on you, in case there was anything you needed?" began Meg.

"How thoughtful, but you know Marjorie takes care of everything for me, she's such a godsend."

Florence had never mentioned a Marjorie before, but the name seemed familiar.

"Marjorie, your cleaner?" quizzed Meg.

"Yes, dear, but she's much more than just a cleaner. Saint Marjorie I call her, looking after me and several others like she does."

"Thats so kind. Who else does she look after?" enquired Meg.

"Well Celia, she's an invalid you know, stroke victim, poor thing." Obviously news of Celia's death had not yet reached Florence Darby's insular existence. Meg said nothing as Florence continued, "Then there's the blind man, I always forget his name, and she used to take care of the Pipers."

Meg's ears pricked at the mention of the couple's name.

"The Pipers, are you sure?"

"Yes, dear, she's Eva's sister."

Meg thought for a moment. "I thought the Pipers had no family?"

"She was adopted by Eva's parents and came to live with the Pipers years ago. That's what I heard. She's a regular Florence Nightingale," giggled Ms Darby.

Meg was suddenly diverted from the reason for her visit. Marjorie needed to be interviewed; she could be the key to unlocking the ever-growing puzzle that was the Pipers.

"Where does Marjorie live?" queried Meg.

"Now that I don't know," answered Florence. "She lived with the Pipers until her marriage, but I don't recall where she moved to. She married Frank Kimble, he was a local lad. She can't live far away, she's always visiting the avenue and she walks everywhere, she doesn't drive."

"Is she still married?"

"Widowed, dear, poor Frank died shortly after their wedding. Marjorie's been on her own ever since."

Florence Darby was an interesting old lady with more stories than Rudyard Kipling, especially when she was having a lucid day and her memory served her well.

"There's something I need to ask of you, Florence," began Meg solemnly.

"What is it, dear?"

"I'd like to take some of your DNA for testing."

Florence stopped mid-pour. "What for, dear, do you think I'm sick? Am I going to a home for the elderly?"

"Not at all, but I have some evidence that may help us find out what happened to your son, Marcus."

Florence almost dropped the China teapot. Meg steadied her hand and completed the task.

"My son?" She trembled, not quite sure how to deal with the news.

Meg waited for a moment, allowing Florence to gather her thoughts.

"A simple swab on the inside of your cheek is all I need. What do you think, will you do it?"

Florence took a nibble from the side of her scone. "Is he alive?"

"I can't answer that question at the moment, but I'm hopeful that I can trace him."

"In that case, yes, I'll do it," agreed Florence, wiping a blob of cream from the end of her nose.

"I'd also like to take your fingerprints?"

Florence eyed Meg suspiciously.

"Are you arresting me, or setting me up for a crime I didn't commit?"

"Oh, Florence, you've been watching way too many movies," laughed Meg.

***

Rosemary Swann had exhausted every avenue in her search for the existence of the boy, Marcus. Apart from his short visit to A&E he appeared to have vanished from society.

"He didn't go to school, or college, or uni. I can't find his name attached to any business, he doesn't appear on the BMA register nor the ICAEW. He doesn't have a passport or social media. I just don't know where else to look," she moaned as Meg appeared beside her desk.

"I do." Meg grinned. "Start looking for Marjorie Kimble, married to Frank. Lives in the area, in fact lived with the Pipers. She was Eva's younger, adopted sister, apparently. If Marcus lived there at the same time she will surely remember him."

Rosemary beamed with renewed vigour and set to work immediately.

CHAPTER 30

Marjorie Kimble had witnessed the boy's abuse first-hand. She'd been privy to it herself before he came along.

The Pipers were a callous couple, devoid of emotion or affection. Edward Piper had an unhealthy interest in children, a fact that Eva conveniently chose to ignore.

Marjorie observed the steady flow of children that passed through the household, the tear-stained faces of infants plucked from society, parted from their families and plunged into a world they would hope not to survive.

Marjorie had been one of those children, but she'd learned to play the game. She gained the Pipers' trust, earning her the eventual right to her own bedroom. She did as she was asked and never complained, even when Edward visited her in the darkness of the night.

Marcus was just a baby when the Pipers removed him from his pram outside Florence Darby's house. All that remained of his previous life was a silver rattle, trimmed with blue ribbon, embroidered with the letter M.

She watched Marcus grow, saw the effects of continual abuse slowly devour him. Imprisoned in the basement of the house, he was fed scraps from their table, and drank his own urine to quench his thirst. His skin flaked and peeled from lack of vitamins and sunlight, and his bones poked sharply beneath the translucency of his pale skin.

How he had survived Marjorie did not know, but survive he did. Marjorie did her best to sneak him food and water, she read to him when the Pipers weren't at home and sang to him when he cried. Marcus was the closest she had to a brother, to family. As he grew so too did the hatred he felt for his captors. Their cruelty infested his psyche and over time he transformed from a sweet, scared little boy into a vengeful, bitter monster. His mind shattered by the psychological battle that raged within and Marcus could no longer differentiate between the world he had created in order to survive, and the reality of the world in which he lived. He was fractured, he was insane.

As he developed the strength of manhood he was able to overpower the ageing Pipers and escape his depraved existence. What became of him Marjorie didn't know, but she knew he was back, the Pipers' murders confirmed it.

As the years passed Marjorie became Florence Darby's carer. She hadn't the heart to admit that she had grown up with Marcus in the house next door, though she wanted desperately to make amends for the guilt she felt and caring for Florence seemed the only plausible option.

CHAPTER 31

In Dublin, Eddie O'Shea had been taken in for questioning. His involvement with Hamelin Holdings and the payments he made to the Pipers were of most interest, but O'Shea, accompanied by his expensive lawyer made no comment through the entire interview and was released hours later.

***

Boyd O'Leary appeared on the radar of border police as he entered England, this time in a new Transit van. He was detained and picked up by Briggs and Grayson and brought to Aberbarry.

***

Meanwhile, Ewan Davis had located the directors of Hamelin Holdings. It seemed that Eddie O'Shea was only one of them, Jasper Rockwell and Arabella Constantine being the others.

"Jasper Rockwell, the newspaper guy?" questioned McGurn.

"Yes, sir, the very same," replied Constable Davis.

The mention of the Rockwell name caught Meg's attention. Elliot's father mixed up in something as sordid as child trafficking seemed implausible, though she had never met Mr Rockwell Senior.

"And the woman, Arabella... what do we know about her?"

"Very little at the moment, sir, she seems to be more of a silent partner," advised Davis.

"That's as may be, I want to know all about her. If she's helping to fund this company then she's as guilty as the rest."

"Meg should be sent to question Rockwell," suggested Fin from the back of the room.

"Why's that?" queried McGurn.

"She's seeing his son," came the reply.

It was a low blow even for Fin, and Meg blushed uncontrollably as the room turned to stare at her.

"Is this true, Quinn?"

"Not exactly, sir," fumbled Meg, trying desperately to fight back the tears of Fin's betrayal. "I made contact with Elliot Rockwell over the headline he had put out about the child pose killer. We've become friends, that's all."

"Sounds like more than friends to me," scoffed DC Briggs as the room erupted into laughter.

"Grow up!" McGurn demanded, seeing the look of horror on Meg's face. "Perhaps you could use your friendship to do a little digging?" prompted the DCI gently.

Meg nodded. Fin had sealed his fate. She threw a disdainful glance towards him as a solitary tear caressed her cheek.

Fin hung his head regretfully, unable to make eye contact.

Patrick Grayson took control of the situation, whisking Meg aside. "Take the day off, Meg, McGurn will understand."

"No," commanded Meg, "I won't give Fin the satisfaction."

"In that case Boyd O'Leary is being escorted to interview room 3, if you'd care to join me?"

Boyd O'Leary was in his mid-thirties, short in stature with blue eyes and strawberry blond hair. He had the most angelic face and at first glance appeared nothing like the portrait McGurn had painted.

"Don't be fooled by the baby face," muttered Grayson as they entered the room.

Boyd rose from his seat as Meg appeared, a polite and old-fashioned-style gesture.

"Pleased to meet you, miss." He offered his hand and smiled sweetly.

Meg shook it cautiously, awaiting the appearance of horns and forked tongue.

"Your halo's slipping," scoffed Grayson, taking his seat.

"Now, now, Officer, so sceptical," scolded O'Leary with a soft Irish brogue. "I'm cruising the highway of reformity."

"Well that's a good thing, Mr O'Leary, you'll be answering my questions honestly then?"

"Of course. Nothing but the truth, Your Honour," he joked.

Grayson produced a photograph of the blue van.

"You were driving this vehicle on Tuesday last?"

"If you say so, Officer."

"I do say so, here you are at the docks. That's you, isn't it, sitting behind the wheel?"

Boyd scrutinised the image carefully. "Indeed it is."

"What were you doing in Wales that day, Mr O'Leary?"

"My job, Officer."

"And what is that?"

"Whatever the boss tells me it is," came the reply.

"When you say boss, are you referring to Eddie O'Shea?"

"Yes, that's correct."

"What had Mr O'Shea asked you to do that day?"

"Pick up some kids from a farmhouse and transport them back to Dublin."

Boyd was surprisingly co-operative as Grayson pressed on. "Why were you picking up children and taking them to Ireland?"

"Why? Cos I was told to."

"You didn't question, just picked them up and ferried them across the sea?"

"I'm not paid enough to question," replied Boyd, "I just do as I'm told."

"So when you get back to Dublin with the children where do you take them?"

"To the yard."

"And where do they go from there?"

"Now that I cannot tell you."

"Can't or won't?"

"Can't, Officer, I have no idea what happens next. I get paid for the delivery and go home to my wife." O'Leary grinned.

"Do you have kids?" asked Meg, speaking for the first time.

"Yes, two."

"So as a father of children yourself, are you not the least bit curious as to what happens to the 'delivery', as you call it?" she continued.

"No, miss. I never have contact with them, see, someone loads them into the van in Wales and someone else unloads them in Ireland. I never actually see them."

Meg removed the image of Tyla Cassidy and placed it on the desk.

"Do you recognise this little girl?"

"No," replied Boyd after briefly glimpsing the photograph.

"Well this little girl is Gerald Cassidy's granddaughter. That makes her your half cousin? She was in the last delivery you dropped off. She shouldn't have been, she was a mistake and Mr Cassidy wants her back."

It was a dangerous tactic using the Cassidy name, but Meg wanted to know whether Boyd felt threatened by it and whether his answers had been truthful. Her answer came in the form of a horrified expression that lit O'Leary's face at the mention of the infamous family.

"A Cassidy you say, holy shit. I don't know nothing about that. Gerald's granddaughter?"

Meg nodded and glanced towards Grayson.

"You say O'Shea is your boss?"

"Yeh," replied Boyd, still unnerved by the recent revelation.

"Who's O'Shea's boss?"

Boyd thought for a moment, as if the question were designed to trick him. "There's no one above, Mr O'Shea," he mused. "Eddie's the gaffer, the big cheese, call him what you want."

"Do the names Jasper Rockwell and Arabella Constantine mean anything to you?"

"No, should they?"

"Mr O'Leary, I want you to go back to Dublin and find out where Gerald Cassidy's granddaughter is. That just might save your life," threatened Grayson.

"My life? Why my life?" gasped Boyd, sweat forming across his brow.

"Because when Gerald finds out you took his granddaughter to Dublin in the back of your van, he's going to come looking for you," threatened the DI, knowing full well that Gerald Cassidy was currently in detention.

"Be very careful with your threats, Detective," scolded O'Leary's lawyer. "You're crossing a line."

"Yes, sorry," replied Grayson, aware that his statement had already produced the desired impact. "Here's my card, ring me at any time, Mr O'Leary," nodded Patrick with a smirk of satisfaction.

The detectives rose and left the room.

"We've got him riled, let's put a tracker on him. I'm certain he will lead us to the children," proffered Grayson.

"Good job, Inspector," praised Meg, patting his shoulder. "It appears O'Leary is far more afraid of Gerald Cassidy than Eddie O'Shea."

"That's what I was counting on."

Briggs was chosen to follow O'Leary at Meg's request. She viewed it as adequate penance for his ill-timed comment in the briefing room earlier. That would leave Fin working solo for a while.

Meg left the station. She had a date with Elliot Rockwell.

CHAPTER 32

Elliot arrived at Della's in a convertible sports car.

Meg was waiting and jumped in beside him. "Where are we going?" she queried.

"A little place I know about twenty miles away," he answered. "You look beautiful, by the way," stated Elliot with a huge smile.

"Thanks, but I've had to borrow these off Della and she's a tad slimmer than me," replied Meg, feeling the pinch of discomfort around her midriff.

Elliot was looking extremely handsome. He wore his clothes like a fashion model, his hair was always impeccably styled and his eyes sparkled radiantly in the glow of oncoming headlights.

"What changed your mind?" he questioned.

Meg hesitated. Truthfully she was on a mission for her DCI, but then Fin's behaviour had made her question their future, and at the moment it looked pretty bleak. Elliot had been nothing but nice, and she couldn't deny that she had feelings for him.

"Honestly, I missed you," she answered with a smile, though she knew she wasn't being completely truthful.

"I missed you too." He grinned, reaching for her hand, squeezing it gently.

They reached their destination, a beautifully thatched dwelling, sitting in acres of countryside, approached along a tree-lined driveway.

"This looks beautiful," announced Meg, stepping out of the car. "It looks like someone's home."

"That's because it is," replied Elliot with a wry smile. "It's my family home."

He led Meg to an artisan door that opened into a panelled hallway. A large, ornate staircase rose upwards announcing a galleried landing above.

"This is amazing," sighed Meg, touching the artistry of the woodwork. The musk of aged timber combined with the wax of its fortified lustre triggered a memorable aroma. Meg was suddenly thrust into the mansion house as a flood of images flashed before her.

"Are you okay?" queried Elliot.

"Yes, I'm fine. I used to spend a lot of time in a house like this, it's brought back memories, that's all," she explained, omitting the murderous events that occurred there, which had haunted her life ever since.

"Come, let's go through to the living room," suggested Elliot.

They sat beside an open fireplace feasting on freshly chopped logs. The room was delicately shaded with pastel tones and accessories, the signs of a woman's touch evident by the additional throws and profusion of flowers.

"You live here alone?" questioned Meg.

"No, with my mother, father and sister-in-law."

"You have a brother?"

"Had," sighed Elliot. "Magnus, he died in a car accident a couple of years ago. His wife survived, and as she has no family to speak of, she was offered a home here."

"I'm so sorry," stuttered Meg. "I had no idea."

"It's fine, Meg, how would you know?" soothed Elliot.

"Are they here? Can I meet them?"

"Not this time. Father's away on business and so the girls have headed to a spa for a few days. Don't worry, though, you'll meet them, I promise."

The doorbell rang unexpectedly, Elliot raced to answer its call and appeared holding two bags of gourmet food, provided courtesy of his neighbour who was a prestigious chef and ran a takeaway service for a select clientele.

The food was delicious, each course paired with appropriate wine, finishing with brandy and handmade chocolates beside the fire. Elliot brewed coffee and they chatted away the evening into early morning, finally falling asleep entwined in each other's arms.

As the light of a new day prodded them into consciousness, Elliot showed off his culinary skills with the production of fluffy scrambled eggs and bagels.

"I can't believe we fell asleep," mused Meg, tucking into the breakfast delight.

"I really am that boring!" joked Elliot. "If you want to take a shower before we head off you can use my room."

Meg welcomed the chance to refresh and free herself from the bounds of Della's tight-fitting dress. Elliot offered her jeans and a jumper from his sister-in-law's wardrobe.

"She won't miss them," he proffered. "She has so many it would be impossible for her to detect the loss."

Elliot's room was untidy, dominated by a huge television and several couches. He owned an elaborate vinyl collection and loved books. The wall of library-style shelving was stacked from floor to ceiling. A gaming chair and console evidence of his youthful side and an oversized bed dishevelled by sleep. There was a single photograph of Elliot with presumably his parents and brother. His mother, elegant with shoulder-length dark curls and his father, the epitome of a country gentleman in the flush of middle age, distinguished and debonair. His brother, older and slightly less handsome, though undeniably his sibling.

The bathroom was marble and mirrored, too many for Meg's liking; a view of her naked body from every angle was not conducive to her self-esteem. She hurried to dress and met Elliot in the hallway.

Stepping out into the daylight Meg was able to view the expanse of grounds that surrounded the Rockwell home. It stretched towards the horizon in every direction, acres of undulating countryside, a haven for deer and wildlife.

"This is so pretty," she stated.

"Yes, I suppose it is, I've grown up with it so I don't notice it anymore."

"That's such a shame."

Minutes later they were speeding towards Aberbarry, leaving the quiet and calm of the countryside and entering the hub of a waking town. Feverish activity already stalked the roads and pavements as the daily routine began, sending adults and children scurrying to their significant destinations.

"See you tonight?" queried Elliot as Meg exited the car.

"Hopefully, maybe you could come round to Della's house, I'll send you the address."

CHAPTER 33

He was irritable, a sure sign that his hunger for small victims needed feeding.

Everything was prepared in case he suddenly appeared with a fresh child, but the police had been hunting the area again, in the aftermath of Celia Tucker's death. If he could keep his habit under control for a few more days, give the police chance to vacate the area, then that would ensure his freedom to pursue a victim again without alerting suspicion.

His self-control was waning fast. It would have been much easier if he'd been addicted to drugs. The boys on the edge of the park supplied a variety of them, he'd seen them dealing hoping no one was watching, but he was.

Marjorie had arrived to prepare lunch. Cheerful, dependable Marjorie.

Hopefully he'd be in a better mood that evening; he was a difficult creature. Thank God he had the shop to keep him busy.

***

Primrose Swann had managed to locate an address for Majorie Kimble. It was an apartment just a couple of streets from Pollard Avenue, which meant she lived within walking distance of her clients.

"That's great news," thanked Meg. "I think I should pay her a visit. Fancy coming with me?"

Constable Swann was more than happy to leave the confines of the station for a couple of hours. Her head buzzed from the incessant undertone of ringing phones, printers, keyboards tapping and constant chatter.

"This should be it." Primrose pointed towards the unkempt exterior of a semi-detached house. The property housed four apartments; Marjorie's was on the top floor, number 3.

Swann pressed the buzzer attached to the woman's name and waited, but Marjorie didn't answer.

A young couple emerged decorated with tattoos and piercings. They eyed Primrose's uniform and rushed on past.

"Excuse me," shouted Meg.

The couple stopped and turned.

"Do you know Marjorie Kimble?"

"Top floor," mumbled the guy.

"She won't be home, though, she's out during the day," added the young woman.

Meg and Primrose settled into the car and waited. Surely Marjorie wouldn't be out all day; she now only had two clients, with the demise of Celia Tucker.

People came and went from the property. The post man called with a parcel, a young girl pushing a pram, and the couple that had passed them earlier, but still no Marjorie.

Then around 2.30 the figure of a woman wandered towards the door, weary looking, laden with shopping bags and dry cleaning.

Meg and Primrose leapt from the car and approached, as she unlocked the door.

"Marjorie Kimble?" queried Meg.

"Yes." The voice sounded tired.

"Mind if we ask you a few questions?" proffered Primrose, displaying her police badge.

"Oh yes, is it about poor Celia?"

"No, actually, it's about your sister, Eva Piper."

Marjorie dropped her shopping bags and staggered forward.

"Are you okay?" queried Meg.

"Just a little light headed," she replied. "I haven't eaten yet and I'm a diabetic."

Primrose took the groceries and Meg helped the woman upstairs and into her apartment. Marjorie collapsed into the nearest chair, deathly pale with rapid breathing.

Primrose offered a glass of water and Marjorie sipped gratefully.

"In my bag," directed Marjorie, "a chocolate bar."

Swann found the treat and handed it over, salivating at Marjorie's every bite of the velvety smooth segments.

Marjorie waited for a few minutes, then removed her coat and proceeded to empty her shopping bags.

"Feeling better?" questioned Meg.

"Much, thank you. I'll put the kettle on."

The apartment was sparse but warm, with a wonderful view of the parkland opposite. Marjorie seemed fastidiously over organised, even performing a simple task like making tea. A form of OCD, thought Meg, to herself. That explained the orderly presence that invaded her home.

Finally, Marjorie took a seat.

"So sorry about that, you caught me at a very vulnerable moment," she explained.

"Glad we were here to help," began Meg. "Now are you up to a couple of questions?"

Marjorie nodded and sipped at her tea cup.

"We wanted to ask you about the Pipers. I believe you grew up in their house?" continued Meg.

Marjorie knew impulsively that this information could only have been divulged by Florence.

"Yes, that's correct, though it's such a long time ago I'm not sure what I can tell you."

"Where there any children kept at the Pipers' during the time that you lived with them, other than yourself of course?"

"Children, no, Eva detested them. She only allowed me to stay because we were kin."

"How long did you stay with them?"

Marjorie thought for a moment. She had to get the story straight in her head, she couldn't betray Marcus.

"Oh, I'd be about twelve, I'd say, and I got married at eighteen. That's when I left."

"What were the Pipers like?" enquired Meg, noting that Marjorie's answers were fraught with uncertainty and the underlying hint of fabrication.

"Well, that's difficult to answer. Just like any other couple, I'd say."

"Did Edward like children?"

That question caused a physical reaction, as Marjorie's hand began to shake, spilling drops of tea onto her lap.

"I couldn't say. I think the decision not to have any of their own was mutual."

"Marjorie, were you ever abused by Mr Piper?" blurted Swann. Meg threw her a disapproving glance, but Swann shrugged her shoulders.

Marjorie dithered over the question, her eyes fixed firmly on the tea stains that spotted her skirt.

"Marjorie, can you answer the question please?" Primrose repeated.

The answer came with a barrage of uncontrollable tears as Marjorie mentally relived the times she had felt the touch of Edward Piper's hands beneath her nightdress.

"Marjorie, it's okay, don't upset yourself. Sometimes it's better to talk about these things. We have specialist counsellors who can help you," Meg explained softly.

"I'm sorry," sobbed Marjorie, "it's just that's the first time I've actually allowed myself to admit it."

"I suspected as much," commented Primrose smugly.

"I feel so ashamed," cried Marjorie, reaching for a tissue from the sleeve of her cardigan.

"Nothing to feel ashamed about, but that's how every victim of abuse feels, that's why it's so important to talk about it. It's more prevalent than you may realise."

Marjorie dabbed at her tears. "I don't think I was the only one either," she declared.

"There were others that you know of?" prompted Meg.

"I don't know of them as such, but one day I took a phone call, when Eva and Edward were out. The person at the end of the line mistook me for Eva. The man said, 'Tell Ed, it's on tonight. He can have his pick for the right price.'"

"Did you recognise the man's voice?"

"Yes."

"Can you give us a name?"

"Jasper Rockwell."

"How did you know it was him? Have you met him?"

"Oh yes, he used to visit the house. He spoke with a posh voice and always smelled nice. He always made me feel uncomfortable. I usually stayed out of the way if I knew he was visiting."

Meg and Primrose nodded to each other. Marjorie's words made the connection between Jasper Rockwell, the Pipers and Eddie O'Shea more significant.

"Thank you, Marjorie, you've been more help than you know."

"Poor old girl," declared Primrose as they left Marjorie Kimble's apartment. "Doesn't seem like she's had much of a life."

"Indeed. I think we may have a paedophile ring in our midst, Constable," added Meg.

"I think you might be right," she replied.

"I can't help but think that the child abductions and all these murders are somehow connected," declared Meg.

"What makes you think that?" asked Swann.

"Let's just call it a gut feeling."

CHAPTER 34

Tyla Cassidy had now been missing for two weeks. The child protection agency had so far not detected signs of her or the other children on the dark web. In some ways that was a relief, but in others, it begged the question what had happened to them, and where were they?

The Piper murders had not been solved, nor those of Sable Cain or Celia Tucker, and the child serial killer had not been caught. McGurn was becoming impossible. His frustrations echoed the mood of the station as he called an emergency briefing.

"Right, listen up. About an hour ago I received a call from Inspector Nick Diamond from Somerset CID. He informed me that five years ago he investigated a spate of child murders on his patch. The MO was identical to what we're experiencing. The murders were never solved, but stopped suddenly and he presumes that meant the perpetrator moved out of the area, died or was incarcerated. He gave me the name of their main suspect, Marcus Piper."

The room livened at the mention of the name.

"All we know about Marcus Piper is that he owns the farmhouse used by the Cassidys to store their child victims. We suspect Piper is involved, along with Eddie O'Shea, Jasper Rockwell and Arabella Constantine." McGurn paused momentarily, gathering his thoughts. "Do we have any information on Arabella Constantine?"

From the back of the room, Constable Katie Adler's voice broke the disquiet. "Yes, sir, she's the daughter-in-law of Jasper Rockwell."

Fin threw a glance towards Meg, his lips desperate to declare, 'Thought you'd know that fact.'

"Excellent work, young lady," praised McGurn, his mouth struggling to muster the hint of a smile. "Meg, you had some information you wanted to share." He turned to offer her the spotlight.

"Constable Swann and I interviewed a lady called Marjorie Kimble earlier. She informed us that she lived with the Pipers for a while and that Jasper Rockwell used to visit their home, though she's uncertain as to why. She also declared that she was abused by Edward Piper and she didn't think she was the only one. Her comments hint at an organised ring, well, that's my take on it anyway."

"Where's your evidence?" sneered Briggs.

"I'm working on it," snapped Meg brusquely.

McGurn, sensing the mounting tension stepped forward. "Moving on then, I want us to bring Rockwell and Constantine in for interview and step up the search for Marcus Piper."

McGurn's orders cleared the room.

***

In Dublin Boyd O'Leary had called in a few favours from contacts, desperate to find Gerald Cassidy's grandchild. He'd established that once he dropped off his delivery of children, they made an onward journey to a house a mile from the Irish border. The owner of the house was Eddie O'Shea's sister, Clodagh. What happened next was uncertain, but Boyd was determined to find out.

DC Briggs was hot on his trail and as O'Leary left his home that evening, the detective was waiting.

O'Leary drove for forty minutes until turning off the road, parking and dimming his lights. He exited the car and set off on foot across the open fields with Briggs in hot pursuit. As the glow of houselights flickered in the distance O'Leary stopped and waited, his gaze fixed upon the only homestead in the vicinity.

The wind was biting but Briggs soldiered forward, finally finding refuge in the branches of an old tree. From there he could see the outline of O'Leary lurking in the bushes of the targeted home.

When the lights went out, O'Leary made his move, creeping beneath the shadow of a half moon to a detached garage at the side of the property. Suddenly the glow of torchlight hit the building as O'Leary strained to peer into a side window.

Briggs jumped from his vantage point and made his way to the bottom of the garden. Cloaked by the thickness of the privets, he watched and waited. O'Leary tried the side door of the garage, but a padlock glistened in the twilight, an indication that what was inside was not to be found.

Boyd O'Leary had come prepared, breaking and entering amongst his ever-growing list of criminal skills. Within minutes he was inside. Briggs moved forward, taking cover behind the garage. The house had been quiet until the silence was disturbed by the growling of something large and unfriendly inside. The snarling jaws of a vicious-looking canine appeared at the window of the back door. Briggs moved forward, realising that the unhappy creature had spotted O'Leary leaving the garage. He was carrying something over his shoulder, something small and still.

The dog barked ferociously and the house sprang to life. O'Leary headed for the field, passing Briggs without even noticing his presence. He raced into the darkness with Briggs in pursuit.

The dog had been unleashed and was closing in fast. Briggs stopped running and searched for a heavy object to arm himself. He knew that the jaws of the beast would inevitably find him first.

As the animal leapt towards him he swung the log with the accuracy of an Ivy League batter, catching the dog full in the face. It dropped to the ground, stunned, as Briggs made his escape.

Boyd O'Leary was driving off as the DC reached the roadway and headed for his car. The dog, having recovered from its minor setback was gaining ground. Briggs fumbled for his key fob, unlocking the car as he approached. Safely behind the wheel the dog appeared, salivating and snarling at his window.

Briggs pulled away and drove hastily into the sanctuary of darkness. A half-mile up the road, he called the Dublin police and asked for assistance. If indeed the bundle over O'Leary's shoulder was Tyla Cassidy, then chances were that the other children were also inside that garage. Briggs couldn't leave until he had procured their safety. Boyd O'Leary would have to wait.

The raid on the house was successful. Armed police arrested its occupants and the children found in the garage were safe. Six children in all were carried to freedom. Their mouths taped and their hands and feet bound, but thankfully otherwise unharmed.

Clodagh Breen and her husband Larry were in custody, their own children entering the care system.

Briggs made contact with McGurn.

"That's wonderful news," he declared. "Six children and Tyla, you say. What of the other three?"

What had happened to the remaining children was uncertain. For now they would have to be happy with the outcome of saving the majority.

Boyd O'Leary appeared the following morning at the station in Dublin with Tyla Cassidy wrapped in a blanket.

Meg and Della caught the next flight out as news of her discovery reached them.

***

Tyla was recovering in the children's ward of the local hospital. She was in shock, weak and suffering the effects of hypothermia. Her pyjamas had been removed for forensic examination and she was tucked beneath the sheets of her hospital bed wearing a pink and white night gown, standard issue on the ward.

"Oh, my poor baby," cried Della, sobbing with a mix of emotions as she rushed to her daughter's bedside.

A nurse in dark blue approached.

"Physically she's fine. A couple of bruises and a touch of hypothermia, but other than that and police approval you should be able to take her home in a couple of days," she assured.

"She hasn't been... you know..." asked Della desperately.

"Abused, no."

"Thank God."

"It might take some time for her to recover from this. Just be patient and take it steady. Don't rush her into remembering, leave it to her to talk about it when she's ready," advised the nurse.

Meg knew that as soon as Tyla was able, she would be seen by a trained officer who used toys and dolls to extract delicate information from minors, but she chose to keep that fact to herself.

Meg glanced around the ward. Emotional parents clung to their rescued children, overjoyed at their safe return.

Briggs appeared.

"Well done, Detective," Meg praised, hugging him tightly. "Tully would be proud of you."

Briggs nodded, fighting back the trigger of emotion, his usual bravado displaced by seldom witnessed sensitivity.

"How is she?" he enquired.

"She's going to be fine," replied Meg. "They all are."

Briggs cast a proud eye around the room.

"You did that," stated Meg.

"Not just me. Never thought I'd say it but Boyd O'Leary's actions led to this. He did the right thing for once in his miserable life."

"Yeah, but only because he thought Gerald Cassidy would kill him."

"Well it worked, didn't it?" Briggs smiled. "I'm on the next flight home and a couple of days' leave, just wanted to drop in and see how she was doing."

"It's much appreciated and thank you," Della declared tearfully.

CHAPTER 35

Jasper Rockwell arrived at the station along with Arabella Constantine and a posse of expensive lawyers. He moved with the arrogance of a world leader, composed and dignified, wearing the cloak of inaccessibility. His Etonian background and charismatic demeanour was somewhat intimidating, solidified by the intellectual prowess of his counsel.

Arabella Constantine strode behind him with the grace and elegance of royalty. Impeccably dressed in a black and white suit, wearing leather stilettoes and carrying a designer handbag. They were escorted to separate rooms and offered refreshments.

The lack of evidence attaching Rockwell to any involvement in trafficked children, murders or paedophilia meant his attendance had been purely voluntary.

Meg had been sent to visit Marjorie Kimble again, in the hopes of securing her as a witness if Rockwell agreed to an identity parade.

The DCI and Patrick Grayson entered interview room 1 where Jasper Rockwell sat beside his barrister.

"Mr DuPlessis, you seem to have been visiting us more than usual," began McGurn. "We're not used to the top brass gracing us with their presence."

DuPlessis said nothing. He sat stern and determined alongside his client.

"Mr Rockwell, thank you for agreeing to attend for interview."

"Well if you don't mind, Officer, can we move this along? I have a very busy schedule to uphold," announced Rockwell dismissively.

Calling McGurn 'Officer' was entirely the wrong strategy. If Rockwell had hopes of a quick interview he had just sealed his fate. McGurn would make him sweat as long as he could now, and that could be a very long time.

"Does the name Eddie O'Shea mean anything to you?" queried the DCI.

Rockwell shook his head.

"Are you sure about that, Mr Rockwell?"

"Yes, I'm sure."

McGurn produced an image of the man in question and placed it on the desk.

"You do not know this man?" he demanded, pinning the photograph with his index finger.

Rockwell studied the photo and glanced towards his lawyer for direction. DuPlessis blinked erratically as Rockwell answered, "No comment."

"I find it very difficult to believe that you are in business with a man you have never met. I'm sure a successful man, such as yourself, would be extremely cautious about who he jumped into bed with."

Rockwell remained silent.

"Come now, Mr Rockwell, you're a partner in the man's company, Hamelin Holdings," growled McGurn, his patience beginning to wane.

"I made a monetary investment in Hamelin Holdings, nothing more," came the reply.

"A monetary investment? What exactly does that mean?" McGurn scowled.

"Mr Rockwell is here to answer your questions, DCI, not to explain the reason behind his financial decisions," interrupted DuPlessis.

"He's here to answer any questions I want to ask, Mr DuPlessis, especially when it involves the probable trafficking of children," McGurn snapped.

Rockwell shifted in his seat and grinned at the accusation. "You can't be serious. Do I look like the kind of man who would be involved in the trafficking of children?"

"Why? Is there a special kind of look for men who do that?" barked McGurn. "A man is capable of anything, Mr Rockwell, if it serves his purpose. Now stop playing games and answer the question. Do you know Eddie O'Shea?"

This time Rockwell was truthful. "Yes."

"Thank you," groaned McGurn, rolling his eyes towards Grayson. "If you want a quick interview then may I suggest that you answer the rest of my questions honestly, otherwise we could be here all day."

"On what charge?" queried DuPlessis.

"Child abduction, child trafficking, conspiracy to commit murder, take your pick."

"Steady on, now," scolded Rockwell. "I haven't murdered anyone."

"Got your attention though, didn't I?" McGurn grinned. "So let's start with your relationship with Mr O'Shea. Explain it to me?"

"Eddie and I met through our mutual love of golf. We're both businessmen. Eddie offered me a stake in his company and I accepted."

"And what business is Eddie involved with?"

"Scrap metal."

"Scrap metal, nothing else?"

"Nothing else to my knowledge, no."

McGurn then produced a photograph of Eva and Edward Piper.

"What about this couple? You know them, don't you?"

Rockwell gazed upon the photograph and recoiled, shaking his head in denial.

"Come now, Mr Rockwell, take a closer look. I'm certain you will recognise them," pursued McGurn.

Rockwell shook his head.

McGurn turned towards Grayson as he declared, "Funny, we have a witness says you used to visit the Pipers' home on a regular basis."

Rockwell stirred uneasily, glancing at DuPlessis.

"Stop playing games with me," hissed McGurn, thumping the desk with his fist.

Rockwell appeared decidedly unnerved; the DCI had rattled his composure with the mention of a witness.

"Yes I did know the Pipers, but a long time ago," he revealed, exasperated.

"Then why deny it?"

"I'd heard of their murders and I didn't want to be implicated," expressed Rockwell.

McGurn studied the fractured façade of Rockwell's cool exterior and decided to call an auspicious interval.

***

Meg caught Marjorie Kimble leaving Florence Darby's home.

"Mrs Kimble," she called, but the woman either didn't hear or was ignoring her.

Meg quickened her pace as Marjorie crossed the road to the blind man's house and caught up with her as she reached the driveway.

"Mrs Kimble."

Marjorie turned begrudgingly as Meg approached.

"Just a quick question," gasped Meg, catching her breath. "Would you be willing to identify Jasper Rockwell in an identity parade?"

Marjorie's face paled at the mention of the man's name again.

"Please, Mrs Kimble, it could really help save other children from similar experiences to yours," begged Meg.

Marjorie pondered the request momentarily. "Would he be able to see me?" she questioned.

"No, you would be in a different room looking at him through a special window. You will see him, but he won't be able to see you."

"In that case, yes," agreed Marjorie.

Meg wanted to hug her for her bravery, but the woman appeared so feeble that a hug may shatter her.

"Thank you, Mrs Kimble. I will let you know when you're needed."

***

In interview room 3 DS Finlay Castleton and PC Ewan Davis sat opposite the alluring Arabella. There was no denying the woman was attractive, though Castleton suspected that behind the outward beauty she concealed a black-widow-type personality.

"Ms Constantine," he began.

"Arabella, please, Sergeant," she enforced.

"Arabella, you're here to answer questions about your involvement with this man, Eddie O'Shea." He pulled the image of the Irishman from his folder and placed it in front of her.

She eyed it from the security of her chair and passed it across to Gregory DuPlessis, her lawyer.

"My involvement is merely that of business. I have barely even met this man except for a couple of unfortunate occasions," she explained.

"You say unfortunate, why?"

"Because I had no desire to meet the deplorable little man. He is of no consequence to me."

Arabella was emotionless, the trait of the black widow becoming more evident.

"But you are a shareholder in his company?"

"I am, that is correct, though how I allowed myself to be cajoled into such status I cannot imagine. I can only think that Jasper caught me in a vulnerable moment."

"So you're saying it was Jasper Rockwell who coerced you into becoming a partner?"

"Why else would I have dealings with such a man?" she scoffed defiantly.

"Did you invest money in O'Shea's company?" proffered Castleton.

"I did, quite a large sum too."

"And what kind of company did you think you were investing in?"

"Scrap metal. Well, that's what Jasper said. Why? Is it something illegal? Is that why I'm here?" she purred.

"Jasper Rockwell told you you were investing money in a scrap metal business, is that correct?"

"Yes, Hamblin Holdings or something to that effect."

"You know nothing of the child trafficking?"

Arabella almost keeled over; her shock was sincere. She steadied herself, her hand visibly shaking as she gripped the metal edge of the desk tightly. For a moment, the vulnerable side of Arabella made a fleeting appearance until composure regained control.

"Did you know about this, Gregory?" she demanded, suddenly putting her lawyer in the spotlight.

Gregory DuPlessis shied from the question with a shrug.

"I bloody well hope not," she hissed. "Just wait until I see Jasper. How dare he involve me in something so despicable? I always sensed he had an unhealthy interest in young people. Porn is one thing, but trafficking is entirely unforgivable."

Arabella Constantine was visibly distraught; the thought of child trafficking had disgusted her. "Magnus and I were desperate for a child. His untimely death put a stop to that. I love children, I could never allow myself to knowingly play any part in harming them," she protested.

Castleton believed her. Her reaction was too real not to. He understood the pain of losing a child. He recognised the signs of legitimate emotion, he'd seen the same expressions in his wife's face.

"Ms Constantine, you're free to go," he declared. "Thank you for your time."

Castleton closed his file and left the room.

McGurn was about ready to reconvene his interview with Jasper Rockwell, when he received a call from Dublin Police. Eddie O'Shea had struck a deal to secure himself a minimum jail sentence by whistleblowing on his accomplices. He named Jasper Rockwell as not only the money behind Hamelin Holdings, but the brains behind their clandestine operation and the instigator of the child trafficking sideline.

Clodagh Breen had implicated her brother, O'Shea, stating he merely used her garage for storage, though she denied any knowledge of the stored items being children. The fact that the children were brought food and bottled water during their stay at her isolated property did not entirely validate her evidence. She was more than happy for O'Shea to shoulder the blame whilst pleading plausible deniability for herself and her husband.

In turn, O'Shea found his voice and implicated Jasper Rockwell and a group of his upper-class associates, which included judges, lawyers, and MPs as the real force behind the trafficking racquet.

"He pampered to their salacious appetite for young children," stated O'Shea, who denied sharing or partaking of their interest. "I merely delivered the goods and that's where my involvement stops."

McGurn contacted Meg and asked her to pick up Majorie Kimble. He had enough to place Rockwell in an identity parade, whether he agreed to it or not.

At the same time, Castleton and Davis were on their way to Rockwell's home with a search party and warrant.

CHAPTER 36

Tyla Cassidy arrived home to a vibrant display of balloons and 'welcome home' banners.

The little girl was physically fine, but the trauma of her experience was evident in her inability to verbally communicate. Whether this development was from choice or shock was uncertain.

It was decided by McGurn that she be allowed to spend a few days adjusting to life at home before being questioned by the police. It was possible that Tyla knew the whereabouts of the other three children and that she could provide significant information.

Joel had arranged Tyla's dolls and cuddly toys around the table and laid out a feast of sandwiches and cupcakes including all of his sister's favourites. Tyla seemed excited by his efforts and joined the tea party.

She watched her favourite cartoons on TV and slept the afternoon away in the safety of her mother's arms.

Meg needed to return to work, as she'd promised Marjorie she would be present when she undertook the identity parade.

Six men entered the room and stood against the wall. Each was asked to step forward by their given number. Marjorie remained silent and still until number five, Jasper Rockwell, moved closer into view.

Marjorie began to tremble as she pointed an accusing finger towards the mirrored glass.

"Do you recognise that man?" queried McGurn.

"Yes," replied Marjorie, "that's Jasper Rockwell."

"Is he the man who visited the Pipers' house when you lived there?"

"Yes," she muttered, trying desperately to control her emotions.

"Thank you, Mrs Kimble, you've been extremely helpful," praised McGurn. "Quinn, you may take Mrs Kimble home."

The journey was silent.

"Here we are, home again," announced Meg, stopping outside the semi-detached property that housed Marjorie's apartment. "You did great today, I'm very proud of you."

Marjorie's eyes pooled with tears as she slowly turned in Meg's direction. "That's the nicest thing anyone has ever said to me, thank you."

Meg felt the stir of emotion as she watched the woman disappear inside. What a sad life Marjorie must have had and what a sad and lonely existence she now lived.

Suddenly, her phone rang – it was Elliot. He'd been calling all morning, and she'd ignored him, firstly because she had been so busy and secondly, because she knew he was calling about his father.

"Hey, sorry, I've been knee deep in it today," she explained.

"Knee deep in it with my father," bawled Elliot without hesitation. "What the hell is going on, and why didn't you have the decency to tell me?"

"I cannot divulge confidential police information. I'm not a snitch like your mate Alex," replied Meg sarcastically.

"No, you're not. It's a good thing he rang me otherwise I wouldn't have known what was going on."

Meg was displeased with Elliot's tone but she chose not to engage in petty exchanges.

"They're searching our home, Meg, Mother's beside herself. Can't you tell me anything?"

"Your father is being detained on serious charges, Elliot, that's all I can say. Anything else you want to know I suggest you ask Alex."

The dial tone replaced his voice. Elliot had hung up.

***

Jasper Rockwell had been detained, along with the DuPlessis brothers who themselves had been named as conducive associates to Rockwell's trafficking business.

The search of the Rockwell property was insanely helpful, his computer and laptop providing a significant list of names and addresses of what could only be described as members of a paedophile ring, as well as dozens of pornographic images and videos of children.

Transactions credited to Eddie O'Shea appeared to be for the use of his vehicles and staff. Eddie then deposited a meagre offering in his sister's account for the use of her property.

Transactions to the Pipers and their involvement were yet to be clarified, but the money came from Hamelin Holdings, some of which they used to pay Gerald Cassidy.

"What a tangled web," declared McGurn, studying the file in his hand, "but good job, everyone. Key members of society are being arrested as we speak. It seems we have stumbled upon a paedophile ring of huge proportions. Preliminary indications show it stretches far and wide across Europe and beyond."

The office erupted with cheers and claps, as McGurn absorbed the tumultuous roars of praise.

"Let's not get ahead of ourselves," he calmed. "We still have unanswered questions, but from the evidence so far, I'd say Rockwell and his cronies are heading for a lengthy stretch."

"Pompous bastard deserves it," roared Ewan Davis.

"Yes, thank you for your input, Constable." McGurn grinned. "Even pompous bastards are not above the law."

The room erupted with laughter.

"Listen up now," commanded McGurn, repressing the momentary lapse of frivolity. "The Pipers. We still don't know where or how they fit in with Rockwell and gang; we need to find out. The murders of them, Sable Caine and Celia Tucker remain unsolved. If they are connected I want to know how. The whereabouts of Marcus Piper is still unknown, find him and lastly, and perhaps most time sensitive are the child murders. We cannot afford for the child post killer to strike again. So let's get down to business."

Meg was pulled to one side by McGurn. "Your witness, Marjorie... err. She lived with the Pipers?"

"Yes, sir, until her marriage."

"Did she ever mention any other children living in the house?"

"No, sir, I asked about that and she denied it."

"The rattle you found embroidered with the letter M, any thoughts?"

"Personally, I think the Pipers abducted Marcus Darby, their neighbour's child. The rattle belonged to him."

"Have we searched for Marcus Darby rather than Piper?"

"Yes, sir, his mother never registered the birth. It was an era when unmarried mothers were frowned upon."

"Ahh, yes I see." McGurn's brow furrowed deeply, something he did when he was lost in thought. "Perhaps it would be helpful to visit Marjorie again. Put a little gentle pressure on. I think your witness knows more than she's telling."

"I agree, sir. Might I suggest DS Castleton take the lead on that? He's extremely adept at getting women to talk."

McGurn nodded, unaware of Meg's hidden innuendo, and signalled Castleton.

CHAPTER 37

He was hunting. He watched the steady stream of school children pass his shop window. Some stopped to admire his jewellery with their mothers, their eyes glowing at the sparkle of precious gems that graced his display.

He wanted to run outside, grab the closest child by the arm and haul it into the depths of his secluded workshop. His appetite was becoming ferocious, almost uncontrollable, and such that his usual carefully executed plans were becoming insignificant in his thirst to kill. The exhilaration of extinguishing life gave meaning to his own existence. Breathing in the power and the dominance that his addiction produced, a momentary glimpse of euphoria, just like drugs, his was an addiction that it was impossible to live without.

When the urge became so strong there was nothing he could do to control it, except succumb to its demands.

***

Primrose Swann arrived at Della's home with a bag full of therapeutic toys. Tyla was making good progress. She'd uttered the odd word, but her speech was still dramatically disabled. Tyla had refused to sleep in her own room or even play in there, choosing to sleep with her mother instead.

Primrose suggested redecorating might be a good idea, with Tyla picking the colour scheme. A change of bed linen might help the little girl disassociate the night of her abduction with the current design, all sensible and practical advice.

"Hi, Tyla." Primrose smiled, entering the kitchen where the girl was playing on the floor.

Primrose wasn't dressed in uniform, she'd opted for a more casual look in jeans and jumper. Tyla was more likely to respond if she didn't have to look beyond the status of a uniform.

Della put the kettle on as Primrose attempted to make herself comfortable on the floor beside her daughter. Tyla managed a smile, as the oversized bottom of Primrose Swann hit the ground with the grace of a baby elephant.

"Oh, that wasn't an easy manoeuvre," gasped Primrose, panting for breath. "What are you playing, sweetheart?"

Tyla picked up a doll and offered it to her new friend.

"Thank you." Swann smiled. "My name is Primrose and I know your name is Tyla, but what's this little girl's name?" she asked, staring at the doll.

Tyla didn't respond.

"Perhaps she doesn't have a name," queried Primrose. "In that case I think we ought to give her one, don't you?"

This time Tyla nodded enthusiastically. Primrose smiled reassuringly towards Della, who was watching and listening from the kitchen.

"What shall we call her then? Everyone should have a name, shouldn't they Tyla?"

Tyla agreed with a shake of her head.

"How about we call her Mary?"

Tyla complied.

"Okay, let's put Mary there next to you and let me introduce you to some of my doll friends."

Primrose produced three small rag dolls. Each face was different, displaying a range of emotions.

"This is Amelia," began Swann, "she's smiling because she's happy. Are you happy, Tyla?"

Tyla nodded in agreement.

"Let me see your biggest happy smile," encouraged Primrose.

Tyla smiled widely, the tips of her white teeth just visible beneath the lips.

"What beautiful teeth you have," commented Primrose, "I would never stop smiling if I had teeth like yours," and she pulled a funny face.

Tyla laughed heartily. Primrose was making a connection.

The next doll was smiling, but not as brightly as the one before. Primrose introduced her as Jenny.

"Jenny isn't quite as happy as Amelia today, do you want to know why?"

"Yes," whispered Tyla.

"Well Jenny got taken away from her mummy and she didn't like that very much."

Tyla's face turned serious as she listened.

"Have you ever had to leave your mummy, Tyla?"

Tyla looked at the floor sullenly.

"It's okay, she's back with her mummy now, that's why she's smiling," continued Primrose, conscious of damaging the newly formed bond.

Primrose sipped at her tea, giving Tyla the chance to play with the new dolls. She knew that the last doll would make the biggest impact; it had been given the name of one of the missing children who was known to have spent time with Tyla in the bedroom at the farmhouse, but wasn't found in the garage near the Irish border.

"How's she doing?" whispered Della.

"She's doing great. This is a lengthy process. It's all about gaining the child's trust and them feeling safe enough to open up. Sometimes it takes multiple sessions, but so far, so good. Don't worry, Della, Tyla's making good progress."

Primrose finished her tea and began interacting with Tyla and the dolls she had already introduced. When she felt the time was right she produced the last doll who had been cleverly clothed in the colours that the abducted child had been wearing.

"This is Emily," began Primrose.

Tyla eyed the doll precariously; she had recognised the name.

"Emily isn't smiling," stated Primrose. "She can't find her mummy and she isn't happy."

Tyla grabbed her own dolls and hugged them tightly.

"Do you want to give Emily a hug as well?" asked the constable.

At first Tyla shook her head. Primrose hugged the doll to her chest and patted it lovingly. "Poor Emily," she soothed, watching Tyla's reaction. "Can you help Emily?" she questioned.

Tyla sat for a moment, still and thoughtful. Then she reached out her hands and took the doll from Primrose. She hugged it tightly, then quite unexpectedly slapped the doll hard across the face and threw to the floor.

"Oh dear, what happened? Did Emily upset you?"

"No," replied Tyla. "Emily doesn't move." She stared at the doll lying beside her.

"Is that why you hit her, to make her move?" coaxed Primrose.

"Yes," replied Tyla, tears forming in her eyes.

"Why didn't she move?" urged Primrose.

"Because she was dead," cried Tyla as the tears began to fall.

CHAPTER 38

He headed into town as he did every morning to open up the shop. It was a cold, blustery day but the warmth he felt inside did not come from his large overcoat, but from the thoughts of his next victim. Safely caged in the depth of his basement, the child waited for his attention.

He hadn't time to remove his hat and coat when the door opened, an early customer. "We're not open until nine," he announced, checking the wall clock for the time.

"Not a problem, sir, I'm not here to shop," stated the handsome, dark-haired man who approached. "I'm DS Castleton and I'm making enquiries about a watch."

"What kind of watch? I have very few in stock; gems are my passion," he declared.

"I doubt you will have this one in stock, sir." Castleton smiled. "Apparently it's very rare, but I'm canvassing jewellers in the area for information."

Castleton produced the image of a man's hand wearing the watch in question. It was the image Tully had captured on his camera from the stakeout at Sable Caine's house.

He knew the watch instantly, but he pulled out his glasses and studied the image carefully as if he were making its acquaintance for the very first time.

"It looks like an old make, possibly pre-war. There can't be many still in circulation. An heirloom or gift from a deceased relative perhaps. Whoever it belongs to is a very lucky man."

"You have any idea where I might find someone who can tell me more about it?"

"You'll need a specialist, maybe even a dealer in antique jewellery," he suggested.

"Thank you, Mr Simeon."

He didn't correct the officer's assumption of his name. Mr Simeon had been the original owner of the jewellery shop since before the Second World War. When he'd bought it he never got around to changing the name. It was the only shop in town of that type and was lovingly referred to as Simeon's. He decided it was probably best to leave it that way.

That was close. He sighed to himself, removing his heavy top coat and hat. He touched the watch that graced his hand; he never left home without it. Luckily the detective hadn't noticed it concealed beneath the length of top coat, a moment later and it would have been impossible to miss.

***

Castleton drove the short distance from town towards Marjorie Kimble's apartment. The window on the second floor of the dwelling was aglow with light, indicating she was home.

Castleton buzzed for entry and heard the door of the main entrance unlock. The interior of the building was old and badly in need of repair, but like so many landlords, Marjorie's seemed loath to spend money. There was a damp and musty smell, the carpet was dirty and threadbare. The walls cried out for a fresh coat of paint and only one of the two lights that dangled from the ceiling worked. A large patch of mould was forming between Marjorie's flat and the one next door, an asymmetric pattern shaded black.

Castleton knocked; the door opened slightly by itself from the strength of his gesture.

"Mrs Kimble, Marjorie," he called, stepping slowly inside.

The house felt cold. Lamplight glowed by the window, but it was daylight with no need for extra illumination. Perhaps Marjorie had left already and neglected to switch it off.

Castleton moved into the kitchen, where the remains of a half-eaten meal sat on the counter. Two mugs were prepared with coffee beside the kettle, an indication that

Marjorie either had or was expecting company, but neither mug had been used.

The kitchen crossed directly into the living room. It was empty, eerily quiet.

Castleton turned and headed for the bedroom. The bed was neatly made and played host to a striped black and ginger feline. Castleton stroked it gently, reading its collar.

"Hello, Tiger, where's Marjorie?" he muttered. The cat purred and stretched, then resumed its curled position on the warm spot it had claimed.

There was only one room left to explore in this compact dwelling, the bathroom. Castleton turned the handle and peered inside.

There the bloody scene of Marjorie's murder unfolded. She lay in the hollow of the bath tub drenched in her own blood. Gutted from sternum to pelvis in the same way as Sable Caine, Celia Tucker and the Pipers. Castleton stepped backwards and retched for a moment. The contents of Marjorie's torso laid bare, the stench of primary decomposition stale and pungent.

When McGurn arrived, Castleton had regained his composure. He had checked the building for CCTV, but as usual the landlord hadn't installed it.

"Bloody fantastic," cried McGurn. "Our one and only witness slaughtered. I didn't see this coming."

"Looks like she was expecting someone, sir, the two coffee mugs," Castleton pointed out.

"DNA?"

"Unfortunately not, they were never used."

"Get me some answers, Sergeant. Knock on doors, find out if anyone heard or saw anything. Check the street for cameras and the houses opposite," commanded the DCI.

"Yes sir, I'm on it."

Marjorie's neighbours consisted of a drug-addled young couple, a polish woman who spoke little to no English and an old man crippled by arthritis whose hearing was almost non-existent. None of whom admitted to seeing or hearing anything unusual coming from Marjorie Kimble's apartment.

Castleton moved across the road. He spied a house directly opposite that sported an external camera. The owner was home and allowed him to view the footage.

"It's not safe around here these days," protested the lady owner. "I'm here on my own, you know. There are drug users living across the road and what with all these murders, I just don't know what is going on. Aberbarry used to be such a safe place to live."

Castleton was only half listening to her protestations as he scrolled through footage from the previous night.

"Has something happened over there?" she queried, nodding in the direction of the semi that housed Marjorie's apartment.

"I'm afraid so, that's why your camera is so important," declared Castleton. Suddenly he stopped scrolling and watched intently. A man was approaching the property, could he be Marjorie's murderer? Castleton continued to whizz through the evening's footage. If a man went in then a man must have come back out. Around twenty minutes later, the same man left the building. His image was blurry, the camera was not of high quality, but it was a start. Perhaps it could be enhanced at the station.

"I need to borrow this if I may?"

The woman looked at Castleton and then at the hazy figure on the screen.

"Do you recognise him?" queried Castleton.

"I think I do, Officer, but I can't for the life of me understand why. I've seen that figure around before, he's so vaguely familiar."

That was all the woman could say about it, but Castleton left his number in case she remembered anything useful.

CHAPTER 39

The child had wriggled and squirmed, thrown an infantile tantrum and ruined the whole experience for him. When she was dead he felt nothing – no euphoria, no accomplishment, no primordial feelings.

He couldn't stand to look at her; selfish, spoilt little girl. He wrapped her in the shower curtain and returned upstairs.

He'd dispose of her in a couple of days, but he would need another one to replace her. He never afforded two at the same time, primarily because the cage wasn't big enough, but mainly because one distraught child at a time was more than enough to handle. He wasn't as strong as he used to be and he certainly hadn't the patience to cope with more than one at a time.

He hunted, killed and disposed, then waited a while before repeating the cycle. It had worked for so many years, it would be dangerous to change his routine now.

***

The news of Marjorie Kimble's death hit Florence Darby hard.

"I can't believe it, poor Marjorie," she'd cried as Meg informed her of her carer's terrible fate.

Florence did not give one single thought to her own situation, the fact that she had no one to visit her, shop for her, pick up her pills or organise home visits. Meg consoled her with a pot of tea and the distraction of her limited knowledge about the world of trees and plants.

Florence juggled conversation from evergreens to deciduous to Marjorie Kimble's demise.

"Didn't anyone see or hear anything?" she asked.

"No, nothing I'm afraid," replied Meg.

"That's so sad. I can't bear to think of her all alone and no one hearing her cries," declared Florence thoughtfully. "It's just the same with trees, you know."

"Trees?" queried Meg, wary that Florence's dementia was responsible for the unusual statement.

"Yes, dear. It's scientifically proven that when trees are harmed or starved of water they cry, but the sound is too high pitched for the human ear. So when the trees cry they go unheard, just like Marjorie."

***

No sooner had the news of Marjorie Kimble's death hit Aberbarry than a fifth child was found dead at the foot of a tree in the local park. The child had been posed leaning against the trunk with an open book on her lap as if she were simply reading beneath the shade of the old oak.

McGurn was beside himself with frustration.

"Another murder!" he bawled. "That's all I can think about, dream about, read about. I will not allow another murder to happen on my watch." His cheeks puffed and the veins on his temples throbbed; his face was a ruddy purple colour, his head was about to explode from anger.

"He's going to have a heart attack if he's not careful," whispered Swann to Davis.

Davis agreed. DCI McGurn was months from retirement. It was understandable that he wanted to end his career on a triumphant note. No one wanted to be remembered as the commanding officer who didn't solve the crime.

"He'll be leaving in a box if he carries on like this, his blood pressure must be off the scale," declared Swann.

"Come on, Primrose, he needs our help, time is running out."

At the station the image of the man seen entering and leaving Marjorie Kimble's property on the night of her murder had been enhanced. From behind he could have been any man in a coat and hat, however, the footage of him leaving the property was rather more revealing. The man's face was hidden by the peak of his hat, but his left hand and wrist were visible, portraying the same watch that had been captured on Tully's camera.

"Could be coincidence?" proffered Briggs.

"Yes, but I don't think so. The same man is captured on the night of Sable Caine's murder and now Marjorie Kimble's," stated Grayson. "Not only that, he's wearing the exact same watch. This is no coincidence, this is our killer!"

"He must live local," added Castleton.

"This man is our prime suspect until we can rule him out. He's about forty to fifty, I'd say, average height and build. Wears a flat cap and overcoat. Davis, Swann, you're on door-to-door with this image. If he's local someone must know who he is," ordered the DI. "Castleton, stay on the watch. Briggs and Quinn, get down to the archives, dig out any matching murders from the last twenty years and get in touch with Somerset, see if anything matches with the murders they had five years ago. I'm going to speak to Jasper Rockwell."

CHAPTER 40

Tyla Cassidy was making great progress. Her speech had returned and she was ready to start back at school. The sessions Primrose Swann conducted with her led to one conclusion, that the three children who hadn't been found in the garage in Ireland were dead. The circumstances of their deaths were still unknown, but Meg prayed that hypothermia had claimed them and not the hands of a paedophile.

Della waved goodbye to her daughter and returned home. Pangs of separation anxiety haunted the hours as she waited nervously to reclaim Tyla from school.

At 3.30pm she stood beside the main door and watched as a parade of excited, chattering youngsters reunited with family in the playground.

Della's heart was pounding as the last stragglers exited. Finally, Tyla emerged, unaware of the trauma she had unleashed upon her mother.

"Good day?" queried Della, desperately hiding her relief.

"Yes." Tyla skipped alongside her mother as they walked the quarter mile back to home.

On Pollard Avenue the blind man from the house opposite was waiting to cross the road.

"Look, Mummy, that man needs help," pointed out the little girl.

Della crossed and taking his arm said, "Here, let me help you."

"Oh, thank you so much," replied the man. "I could have been there for hours. I have to listen until I'm absolutely certain there is no traffic before I can cross."

"Well you picked the busiest time of day to take a walk," remarked Della.

"How so?" questioned the man.

"School time, it's always way busier than the rest of the day," she declared.

"What's your name?" asked Tyla.

The blind man hesitated. "I didn't realise I had two ladies helping me, how kind. My name is Felix, what's yours?"

"I'm Tyla and I live just there." She pointed her finger, not realising that the man could not see.

Della began to apologise.

"No need," declared the man. "The innocence of youth should never be silenced."

"Why do you carry that white stick?" Della gave her daughter a disapproving look.

"Well I'm blind, you see, the white stick acts as my eyes so that I don't bump into things," explained the man, demonstrating how the aid searched the area in front of him.

"Come, Tyla, let's leave this man alone now," commanded Della, directing her child towards home.

"Thank you again," said the man. "So nice to have met you."

***

Patrick Grayson was waiting in an inner room of the local prison. He was hoping that Jasper Rockwell might shed some light on his relationship with the Pipers, which in turn may lead to the whereabouts of their son, Marcus.

The rattle of keys and clanging of ironwork told Grayson that Rockwell was close.

Jasper entered the room wearing a dull grey outfit. The trinkets of his wealthy lifestyle were gone; no diamond-studded signet ring or expensive Rolex. Stripped of his trophies Jasper was no different from the inmates he shared the prison with.

"Mr Rockwell, please take a seat," began Grayson.

"I thought I'd seen the last of your lot," uttered Rockwell disapprovingly.

"Just a couple of loose ends to clear up and then I promise to leave you alone," declared Grayson.

"What kind of loose ends? Can't it wait until the trial?"

"I'm afraid not. If you'd like me to put a good word in with the judge you'll find it in your interest to co-operate. Besides, your fate is sealed, we have a witness who picked you out of the lineup and she's willing to testify." At that point Rockwell had no idea that Marjorie Kimble was dead.

Rockwell took a seat.

"I just want to know how you knew the Pipers."

Rockwell hesitated and shifted uneasily.

"Look, you and I both know you're probably not to going to leave this place for an extremely long time. What harm will it do to tell me?" proffered Grayson.

"Edward Piper was my accountant. We met nigh-on forty years ago. We hit it off straight away and he became not only my accountant, but my friend. We shared a dark secret, the fact that we both had a penchant for young children. At first we did nothing about it, other than talk in private, but then Edward told me that he had abducted a child and was keeping her in the basement of his home. He offered me access, but I thought it was too risky and too public a place so I declined."

"What was the child's name?"

"Mary, I think. No, Marjorie."

Grayson's mind leapt to the image of Marjorie Kimble lying slaughtered in her bath tub. He knew she had admitted living with the Pipers until her marriage, it had to be her.

"So you never touched Marjorie?"

"No, never. Not that the thought didn't cross my mind, she was a pretty young thing," Rockwell revealed.

"Piper did though, didn't he?"

"I'm certain of it. Couldn't help himself, that one."

Rockwell was excited. An egregious smile crossed his lips, his pupils dilated and his eyes sparkled with desire.

Grayson wanted to vomit, wanted to knock Rockwell from his chair with the power of his fist, but he composed himself and continued.

"What happened next?" Grayson was almost afraid to know the answer.

"We bought a farmhouse – well, Piper did – secluded, off the beaten track, middle of nowhere."

"I get the picture," interrupted Grayson, already aware of its location. "You say Piper bought the farmhouse, but it's registered in his son's name, isn't it?"

"What son?" questioned Rockwell. "Edward had no son, no children."

"Then who is Marcus Piper?"

Rockwell pushed his chair backwards, rocking on two legs as he pondered the question. He began to laugh.

"What's so funny?" scowled Grayson.

"The old dog," laughed Rockwell. "Marcus was a child he abducted for Eva. She had a love-hate relationship with children, but one day she begged him for a baby, so he snatched one for her. She soon became bored of it though."

Grayson detested the way Rockwell referred to the child as 'it', as though he was a disposable commodity, not humanised at all.

"What happened to the boy?"

"From the little that he mentioned, the boy lived in the basement."

"You never saw him?"

"No, I didn't. I do know that one day the child attacked Edward; his face was bruised and a couple of his fingers were broken. When I asked what happened, he said the boy had set upon him and escaped from the house. We never spoke of him again."

"Going back to the farmhouse that Piper bought, you used it to take children there?"

"Yes, that's correct."

"How did you select the children?"

"Well that depended on our clients."

"Clients? What do you mean?"

"Some liked blond hair, some brown, blue eyes and so on."

"So you took the children to order?"

"Essentially, yes."

Grayson felt his stomach leap again. Being in the same room as Jasper Rockwell was nauseating.

"Who abducted the children?"

"That was Eva's forté. She took care of that and Edward drove them to the farmhouse."

"A regular Hindley and Brady operation." Grayson scowled.

"We never killed them," protested Rockwell, with a mortified expression.

"No, you did far worse," growled Grayson. "If you didn't kill them then what happened to them, you let them go?"

"No, we sold them."

Grayson could feel his temperature rise, and the clench of his fist by his side as the words left Rockwell's mouth.

"You sold them to whom?"

"The highest bidder."

Grayson slammed the desk with his fist. "Let me get this straight, you abduct children, take them to the farmhouse, do God knows what to them and when you're finished, you sell them!"

Rockwell appeared confused, as though Grayson's description was perfectly normal and he couldn't see the harm in it.

"We cannot help the way we are made, Detective," he declared.

"No one is made to harm children in the way that you do, Rockwell, it's disgusting, appalling, you choose to do what you do."

Rockwell rose from his seat and banged the door for the warden's attention.

"Sit back down," bellowed Grayson. "I'm not done with you yet."

Surprisingly, Rockwell obeyed.

The warden appeared at the window and Grayson waved him away.

"Right, you abduct the children, you keep them at the farmhouse, when you're finished with them you sell them on, what happens in between those stages?"

"At first we just videoed the children and mailed it to a PO Box for clients to pick up."

"You said 'at first', did that change?"

"Yes, then we got more and more demand for personal contact, so we arranged for clients to visit the farmhouse."

Grayson wiped the sweat from the back of his neck. He wanted to open the nearest window and throw Rockwell through it.

"Is that when Gerald Cassidy and Eddie O'Shea got involved?"

"I suppose it was. The business was so lucrative we couldn't keep up with demand and our clientele were numerous. We found contacts in Europe and beyond. Managing that as well as our own businesses became too much, we had to take on outside help."

"And who better than a couple of gypsies," stated Grayson.

"Gypsies can always be bought for the right price and they have no regard for the law," added Rockwell.

"So Gerald and Reuben abducted the children and kept them at the farmhouse, until transport supplied by Eddie O'Shea picked them up and ferried them to Ireland. What happened next?"

"The children were kept at Eddie's sister's place near the Irish border. From there the children were sold to prospective buyers."

"Get a lot of money for them, did you?"

"A fair amount."

"Paid for your fancy watch and designer suits, put fuel in your Bentley and oysters on your table?" erupted Grayson.

"I assure you, Detective, my newspaper business paid for most of that."

"What was it then, the perverse sexual experience, the power, the dominance? You disgusting, deplorable bastard!"

Grayson unleashed his anger, knocking Rockwell to the ground and pounding on him with all the strength he could muster. Rockwell lay silent, blood oozing from the wounds on his face where Grayson's fists had split the skin and broken his nose.

The warden was there now, pulling Grayson upright, wrestling him away from Rockwell.

"Feel better now, Detective?" Rockwell grinned. "Have children of your own?"

Grayson was panting heavily. He wasn't finished, he wanted to make sure Rockwell never hurt a child again.

Rockwell climbed to his feet, wiping the blood from his eyes. "Never felt the urge, Detective?"

Grayson broke free and crippled Rockwell with a punch to the gut.

"You'll be hearing from my lawyer," grunted Rockwell.

The warden turned to Grayson as Rockwell was led from the room. "I gave you that, it's what every half decent man in this place has wanted to do to Rockwell since he arrived."

"I hope they kill him," replied Grayson.

"Don't worry, Detective, he won't last long." The warden turned to leave. "Oh and this, never happened. I saw nothing."

Grayson nodded appreciatively.

CHAPTER 41

He watched her playing in the bedroom on the first floor, her head bobbing up and down in front of the window, ponytails dancing beside her cheeks. He hadn't noticed her before, or rather hadn't taken the time to.

She would be perfect. His last kill and then a move out of the area; he'd even consider going abroad this time.

He was getting older, he didn't move quite as easily as he used to. A warm climate would suit him nicely. Retirement from the shop should give him a healthy payout and money from the house as well. He would never need to work again. He'd keep up his hobby, though, at least for as long as he was able.

***

Castleton was alone in the office. It was early, he couldn't sleep. Meg had been avoiding him. That bothered him. They needed to sort this out. He still loved her, but wasn't sure she felt the same.

His phone rang. He checked his watch, 7 a.m., should he answer? It would take his mind off Meg.

"DS Castleton, Aberbarry Police," he chimed.

"My name is Esme Rice."

"Yes, Ms Rice, how can I help you?"

"Well I rather thought I could help you, Detective," proffered the voice.

"That sounds intriguing, Ms Rice."

"I live across the road from where that woman was murdered recently. The one in the property that houses apartments."

"Oh yes, the lady with the surveillance camera, I remember."

"That's right. You left your number in case I remembered anything."

"And have you?"

"Yes, the man in the footage coming out of the semi-detached property, I've remembered how I know him."

Castleton grabbed a pen and paper eagerly.

"Okay, Ms Rice, go ahead," he urged.

"He's the jeweller at Simeon's."

"He's Mr Simeon."

"No, Mr Simeon died many years ago. He's the man that bought the shop. I'm afraid I don't know his name but that's definitely him."

"How can you be so sure, Ms Rice? The image was rather blurred."

"It's the watch he's wearing, I recognise it as the one the jeweller wears. It's very old and unusual. I spotted it the last time I was in his shop."

Castleton couldn't thank the caller quickly enough. He left the office like a tornado, knocking Meg sideways in the process but catching her before she hurtled down the flight of stairs that led to the lobby.

"Why are you in such a hurry? You almost killed me," dramatised Meg.

"I'm sorry, but I've just had a tip-off on our suspect."

"Really! I'm coming with you."

Castleton wasn't going to object. They raced to his car and headed for the town centre, but the shop was closed.

"We're too early," sighed Meg. "Have you got a home address for him?"

"Afraid not. We'll just have to wait here until he arrives."

The town centre gradually filled with people, but no one arrived to open Simeon's jewellery shop.

It was 9.30 now, it wasn't looking positive.

Castleton strolled to the window for a hint of the opening times, but there was nothing displayed. He visited the shop next door, a vibrant salon filled with gossiping women and overpowering music. He asked the girl on reception about Simeon's.

"He's usually open when I get here, he's like clockwork, here before 9 and gone before 4," she informed.

"You don't happen to know where he lives, do you?"

"Not a clue, sorry," answered the girl, never allowing her eyes to stray from the nail she was filing vigorously.

"Any idea what car he drives?"

Suddenly, she stopped filing and looked up. "Yeh, he usually parks it round the back next to mine, though some days he walks to work. It's a silver Volvo I think. I'm not great at recognising cars. It's old and there's a stuffed animal on the back seat."

Castleton jumped behind the wheel. "We're going back to the station. I've got his make of car, hopefully we can find him from that."

"What happened to waiting here?" queried Meg.

"The girl next door says you can usually set your clock by him, so if he's not here now chances are he's not coming in today."

"Let's get a search warrant for the shop as well."

McGurn was elated by the breakthrough and even managed a genuine smile.

Katie Adler processed the vehicle information by make, colour and area. Aberbarry was not a large town, but it still produced an astounding eighty vehicles as a match. She reduced that number by removing the cars registered to females, leaving fifty-six. Then she concentrated on a five-mile radius around the shop, leaving only eleven matches.

Briggs, Swann, Davis, Grayson, Meg and Castleton headed out to separate addresses.

***

Meg had no sooner left the building than her phone rang and Della's name popped onto the screen.

"Hey, Della, can't really talk now, think we've got a major lead on our suspect."

Della was hysterical, her words cloaked by sobs and tears. Meg knew something terrible had happened and it involved Tyla. She swung the car around and headed in the opposite direction.

"I'm on my way, Della, stay right there."

Meg arrived at the primary school within minutes, breaking the speed limit several times on her journey.

Della was sitting in the headmaster's office, a snivelling, broken wreck.

"What's happened?" questioned Meg as she rushed to Della's side.

"She's gone again, Meg, my baby has gone again."

Meg searched the face of the headmaster, who beckoned her to one side.

"Tyla arrived at school this morning. She's been ticked off the register, but after playtime her teacher noticed that she was missing from class. We rang Ms Warren to find out whether she had picked her daughter up and forgotten to sign her out. Ms Warren was hysterical, as you can well imagine, especially after everything that's happened.

It appears that somewhere between the start and finish of morning break Tyla has disappeared."

"Have you got any cameras pointing at the playground?" queried Meg.

"Yes, come to my office, you can look at it there," offered the headmaster.

He scrolled to the start of morning break, picking out Tyla skipping by the railings. Moments later she could be seen talking to someone on the other side, but the footage wasn't clear enough to show who. Minutes later, the little girl had vanished from the playground.

Meg rushed from the school and radioed through to Castleton from her car. Then she rang McGurn.

"Sir, we have a missing child. I think she could be the next victim of the child pose killer."

CHAPTER 42

Briggs, Davis and Swann had already eliminated six of the eleven silver Volvos, when they were informed of the missing child. They were told to continue with their mission, whilst Briggs and Grayson were called back to the primary school where the child had disappeared.

"Crazy as it seems, sir, I think our best bet is to interview the children, they might have seen something," suggested Meg.

The headmaster called all students to the assembly hall, suggesting that would be the easiest and quickest way to get answers.

"This morning during breaktime one of our students went missing," began the headmaster. "Tyla Cassidy from class 2. Now listen very carefully, this is very important. Raise your hand if you saw Tyla during break."

A dozen or more hands shot into view.

"Well done, now raise a hand if anyone saw Tyla leaving the playground."

This time only two hands raised.

"Clemence and Astrid, could you come to the front, please? The rest of you are dismissed back to class."

The two young pupils were led to the headmaster's office, where Meg was waiting.

"Come in. My name is Meg and I'm helping the police find Tyla. Now you're not in any trouble, I just need to ask you a few questions, okay?"

The girls nodded timidly.

"Did you see Tyla leaving the playground?"

They nodded consecutively.

"Did she leave on her own or was somebody with her?" smiled Meg.

The smallest child, who also seemed the bravest, raised her hand.

"Yes, sweetie?" soothed Meg.

"She left with a man, I think he was her grandad," muttered the child.

"Okay, why do you think he was her grandad?"

"He looked old."

Meg smiled. That statement when you're six years of age means anyone older than that can be described as old.

"Did Tyla look happy about leaving with the man?"

"Yes, she was holding his hand," replied the girl, whose name was Clemence.

"Have you ever seen that man before?"

"Yes."

"Can you tell me what he looks like?"

The girl paused as if the question wasn't entirely understandable. Her friend, Astrid, joined the conversation, adding, "He was wearing a hat."

"Like a bobble hat?" queried Meg.

The girl shook her head.

Meg searched for hats on her mobile, displaying an array of different varieties, and showed it to the girls. "Any of these hats maybe?"

Astrid shook her head. "It was flatter than those hats."

"Like this?" Meg produced the image of a flat cap.

"Yes, that's it," giggled the child.

"Did you see where Tyla and the man were going? Did they get into a car?"

The girls nodded positively.

"Now let's see how good you are at remembering. Can you tell me the colour of the car?"

They thought for a moment and looked at each other.

"It was white," declared Astrid.

"No it wasn't, it was grey," contradicted Clemence.

Meg felt nauseous as a sudden realisation triggered her instincts. She pulled up the photo of a silver Volvo.

"Is this the car?"

Both girls shouted simultaneously, "Yes!"

The child had been easy to convince. She'd taken his hand and climbed into the car without hesitation. He passed her the cuddly animal, the one he had promised she could hold if she went for a ride with him.

She was to be his last victim in Aberbarry before moving away. She would be special, but not his most special.

He recalled the first child he had encountered. The softness of her hair, the luminance in her emerald eyes. The fact that she loved Jelly Babies. The cuddly toy that now lived on his backseat belonged to her. She had wandered away from her mummy in the shopping centre. He had promised to help find her and said he knew where she lived and would take her home. The child climbed happily into the car clutching the stuffed toy.

At first he hadn't thought about killing her, he just wanted her to experience the childhood he had had. The cage he was locked in at night, the scraps he was fed when someone remembered and the cold that chilled his emaciated body.

The child had screamed as he carried her down to the basement. He had panicked, wary that the neighbours might hear. He had silenced her with a punch of his fist, secured her mouth with tape and locked her inside the cage, the one that had once been used for his dog. He kept her there for a couple of days whilst he decided what to do.

In the end he couldn't let her go, she would lead the police straight to him. He'd spent most of his childhood in a prison, he wasn't going to spend the rest of his life in one too.

That night he took a kitchen knife down to the basement and ended her life. He'd watched hunters slaughter their prey, slitting the torso from the sternum to the pelvis. It seemed apt that he copied their style. After all, he was the hunter and she was the prey.

He hadn't expected to enjoy it so much. It was she who helped him discover the euphoria of rebirth. It was she who set him on the path to self gratification. She was his beginning, his first, his most special.

CHAPTER 43

The last address on Constable Swann's list was actually on Pollard Avenue. She parked at the bottom of the drive. It was empty of a vehicle; perhaps the owner wasn't home. She knocked anyway. A shuffling behind the door and the sound of a faint bark grabbed her attention. A man greeted her, holding a white stick, accompanied by a small terrier.

"Can I help you?" questioned the man.

Swann searched for her ID before realising that it was worthless as the man before her was blind.

"Good afternoon, sir, I'm sorry to bother you. My name is Constable Swann from the Aberbarry division."

"Come in, Officer, don't stand there in the cold," he begged.

Swann stepped inside realising that the question she was about to ask seemed rather insensitive for a person with no sight.

"Are you the registered owner of a silver Volvo?"

The blind man laughed. "I'd love to answer yes to that question, but as you can see I would be rather dangerous behind the wheel of a car."

Swann checked the address.

"This is thirty-nine."

"Yes, that's correct."

"The car is definitely registered to this address," she continued. "You are Victor Stanmore?"

"Ahh, no, Victor's my brother, the car will be registered to him," explained the blind man. "Can I offer you some tea, Officer."

At first Swann declined, but the man encouraged.

"It's gone rather wintry outside. Nothing like hot tea to warm you up," he proffered.

"I take it your brother's not home at the moment then?"

"What makes you say that?"

"The fact that there is no car on the drive."

"Oh, of course, silly me. No, he'll be at work now, gets home around five."

Swann checked her watch. It was only 4.05, almost an hour to wait, but she was warm and about to have tea with a nice, amiable, seemingly lonely gentleman.

"Can I ask where your brother works, sir?" she enquired, sipping at the tea.

"Yes, he has a shop in town."

Swann sipped some more. The man's face turned hazy, her eyes cloaked in a developing mist and the room began to spin.

"Are you all right, Officer?" enquired the blind man.

Swann didn't answer, she closed her eyes and was consumed by darkness.

***

Della was at the police station with Joel, who had been plucked from class extraordinarily early. Katie Adler had been charged with their welfare as Swann had not yet returned to the station.

In the briefing room McGurn rallied the troops.

"Okay, everyone, as you know Tyla Cassidy has been abducted from the school playground this morning. We suspect that the owner of the silver Volvo is our man. Where are we up to with that, Davis?"

"All have been checked off the list, sir, apart from the one Swann was visiting."

"Where is Swann?"

The room buzzed with theories as to why Primrose had not yet returned.

"She's probably enjoying a cream cake somewhere," heckled Briggs.

Davis checked the time. "She should be back, sir, she only had two addresses left to check," he informed, looking decidedly worried.

"What were the addresses?" demanded McGurn.

"Five Parkhurst Street and thirty-nine Pollard Avenue."

The mention of Pollard Avenue threw the room into disarray.

"Davis, get over to Parkhurst Street. Briggs, you take Pollard Avenue," commanded the DCI. "And Briggs, approach with caution."

"Should I go with him, sir?" queried Castleton.

"Aye maybe you should, safety in numbers, but no heroics."

As Briggs and Castleton left the building, McGurn received further information.

"Grayson, Quinn, I need you to visit a psychiatric unit in Cwmdovey. It seems our jeweller spent a stint there, see what they can tell you."

Meg nodded. "Do we have a name yet, sir?"

McGurn studied the piece of paper in his hand. "Victor Stanmore," he replied.

Briggs and Castleton pulled in behind Swann's police vehicle.

"That's her car," commented Briggs. "She could be inside the house."

Castleton radioed for instructions.

"Can you get a look inside the house without making the owner aware?" queried McGurn.

"We'll try, sir."

"Don't attempt to go inside until you have spoken to me," warned the DCI.

***

On the A road to Cwmdovey, Meg and Grayson sped in the direction of Marlborough House, a private psychiatric unit.

"That's it on the left," shouted Meg.

Grayson swung into the car park and claimed his position at the front entrance. A man in dark blue scrubs was taking a smoking break outside. "You can't park there," he yelled.

Grayson ignored him as he and Meg headed for the reception desk.

"Aberbarry Police, I need to speak to whoever is in charge," gasped Grayson, the urgency prevalent in his voice.

The girl behind the desk stared blankly.

"Now, please," yelled the DI. "It's a matter of urgency."

A couple of minutes later a rotund, well-dressed lady approached. "May I help you?" she enquired with a well-spoken accent.

"I need to see the file for this man, Victor Stanmore."

The woman's face drained of colour. The name obviously struck a distasteful chord. "I'm afraid patient confidentiality..." she began to recite.

"Save me the speech." Grayson scowled. "This is a matter of life and death, break protocol and get me that file."

"Follow me," uttered the disgruntled woman.

In the confines of a back office she rifled through a drawer of files, withdrawing the one named 'Victor', and handed it to Meg.

"Did you know him?" queried Grayson, remembering the reaction his name had elicited.

"You don't want to know him," she answered. "Please tell me he's dead or in prison for life."

"He's not dead, but we think he's responsible for the deaths of five people."

"Adults?" queried the woman. "Not children?"

***

On Pollard Avenue, Briggs and Castleton had stealthily approached the house. The curtains of the living room were closed, but the blind that hung at the kitchen window hadn't quite obscured the view. The kitchen was empty, save for a tray on the table which held two cups and saucers, an indication that the occupant had a visitor.

"Okay, there are two possibilities here," whispered Castleton. "She's either gone into another house for whatever reason, or she's still inside this one."

"I'm betting on the latter," responded Briggs.

"Me too, let's inform McGurn and see what he wants us to do."

They crept back to the car, thinking their brief visit had gone unnoticed, but he'd seen them from the bedroom window. He knew it was only a matter of time.

CHAPTER 44

Primrose blinked away the darkness. Where was she?

She couldn't move; her hands and feet were bound and a thick layer of tape covered her mouth.

She wrestled hysterically, the feeling of claustrophobia overpowering rational thought.

A hazy memory replayed in her head. She had been drinking tea with the blind man, when suddenly she was overcome with dizziness, disorientated, falling into darkness. The tea had been spiked and rendered her unconscious.

She was lying on a hard floor, timber planks beneath her, a cold breeze wrapping around her body. She was in a basement.

A noise in the darkness caught her attention. A soft, high-pitched whimpering sound. Was it a dog? She forced herself to roll over, again and again, in the direction of the noise. She rolled onto softer material, plastic, a sheet maybe? Then she hit something solid, metal, vibrating against the weight of her body. The noise was louder now, and close. She touched the object with her fingers, thin metal bars slipping at her touch. It was a cage of sorts and the sound was coming from inside.

Primrose tried to speak through the muffle of restriction, projecting the sound like a ventriloquist, but the words were lost in translation.

She pressed her face hard against the bars, not knowing if she were about to be savaged by a caged animal. Instead she felt the touch of small fingers. A child worked the edge of the tape until her voice was free.

"Don't be afraid, I'm a police officer, I'm going to get you out of here."

The voice whimpered.

"Find my fingers and put your mouth against them, let me remove your tape."

Primrose peeled gently until she felt the touch of young lips and warm breath against her skin.

"That's better, isn't it?" she soothed.

"Yes," sobbed the voice of a young girl.

"I'm Primrose," she declared.

"I'm Tyla," the girl replied.

Primrose froze at the realisation that she was in the basement of the child pose killer.

***

"I don't understand. Who are all these people named here?" queried Meg.

"Those are his brothers," replied the woman.

"He has six brothers?"

"In reality, no, he has none. They are all a figment of his imagination. You see Victor suffers from dissociative identity disorder."

"Is that why he spent time here?"

"He spent time here to avoid a prison sentence. His lawyer pleaded insanity. After six months he escaped, posing as a doctor. We later found the real doctor dead in a storage cupboard, gutted from sternum to pelvis."

Meg and Grayson exchanged a nervous stare.

"You were sceptical of his diagnosis?" quizzed Grayson.

"When you've worked with the mentally ill for as long as I have, it's easy to detect a fraud," replied the woman.

"That's what you thought Victor was? He played these personalities to avoid jail time?"

"That's exactly what he did and he got away with it too," she replied sternly.

"You asked if he'd killed children? Any particular reason?" urged Meg.

"That's what he was on trial for, the abduction and murder of six children. We thought the doctor was just collateral damage, but obviously we were wrong."

"Is there anything you can tell us about him that might help?" begged Meg.

"When he left here, escaped, he was only presenting two personalities, Victor and Felix."

"Was Felix a blind man?" asked Grayson nervously.

"Why yes, he was."

"Oh my god," cried Meg, as the realisation of their killer's identity became clear.

"Thank you for your help, we really need to go."

They rushed from the office. A voice called after them.

"Officers, one last thing. You do know that his real name is not Victor or Felix Stanmore, don't you?"

"What is it then?" demanded Meg.

"It's Marcus Piper!"

***

Pollard Avenue was now a hub of police activity. McGurn had requested armed backup and a hostage negotiator, in the hope of saving Primrose Swann and Tyla Cassidy's lives.

The information Meg and Grayson had gleaned from the psychiatric unit meant that they were dealing with a very unstable and volatile personality. They knew he was capable of murder; the situation needed to be handled with the utmost caution.

Ewan Davis arrived, flustered and concerned for Primrose.

"Aren't you off duty?" quizzed Briggs.

"No one's off duty until I say so," barked McGurn.

The SFOs were already on site and waiting for the negotiator to arrive.

Meg's memory dragged her back in time to a moment she had tried so often to forget. This was the type of operation she and her then-husband, Michael, were involved in. She'd been an armed officer, she knew the dangers facing such a profession. That was how she had lost him. That was the day her life changed forever.

She glanced towards Castleton, he was looking back at her. The hint of a smile crossed his lips. He knew the situation would be difficult for her to observe, he knew the trauma of her past long before she found him in the prehistoric village of Brightmarsh.

In that moment she felt a connection, something she hadn't felt for a very long time. Perhaps there was still hope for them, perhaps they could put their lives back together.

***

In the basement Primrose heard footsteps overhead. She froze, silent and afraid in the dark.

The sound of a heavy object being moved and then the glimmer of light in the distance. Suddenly the room was aglow and the figure of a man was coming down the stairs.

"Very clever, Officer." The man smirked. "Resourceful, I like that."

He was referring to the missing tape and the position of her body.

"I'm afraid I'm going to have to move you back again, you see I need this sheeting for her."

He glared towards Tyla who was huddled in a corner of the cage.

"Please, you don't have to do this... Felix, or is it Victor?"

"It's whoever I choose to be," replied the man with a wry smile. "Felix could never stomach the act, it was always left for me to carry out, but he plays his part too."

"She's only a child. Let her go, take me instead," pleaded Swann.

"Don't worry, Constable, a little patience, please. I'm saving you until last, allowing you a glimpse of what's to come."

He unlocked the cage and fished inside, dragging Tyla screaming hysterically onto the sheet of plastic. There was a collar fitted tightly around her neck biting at her delicate skin, drawing blood beneath its harshness.

Primrose began to shout loudly, banging her fettered boots on the ground.

Victor, unperturbed by the noise grabbed the tape and sealed their mouths. "You can scream and shout all you like, these walls are soundproofed. A bomb could go off and no one would hear it."

Primrose was losing hope, but as the man stooped over Tyla she kicked as hard as possible with her conjoined feet. He fell to one side, almost landing on top of the little girl.

He was angry now and grabbed at the tool box on top of the cage. The point of a sharpened chisel headed in Primrose's direction, piercing her side with ferocity. Pain struck her body with the force of lightning; she writhed from the intensity, tasting the acidity of vomit and metallic trace of blood as they rose into her mouth. She struggled to swallow, knowing that if she didn't she would choke. A steady stream of red liquid flowed from her side, staining the whiteness of her shirt. The tool had missed her stomach, but dissected her kidney. Hope was fading. If she couldn't save herself, she couldn't save Tyla.

Victor withdrew a needle from his pocket and stuck it into the little girl's neck. Within seconds her wrestling, struggling body was still. He stroked her cheek and sniffed at her hair before producing a large, shiny blade.

Primrose closed her eyes. She did not want to witness the demise of the child, any more than she wanted knowledge of her own fate.

As Victor raised the knife in readiness, he was interrupted by the sound of distant buzzing. He turned to Primrose, realising that she had a mobile phone concealed on her person. He patted her body searching for the device, retrieving it from her back trouser pocket and holding it to his ear.

"Marcus, this is Marjorie. Don't hang up, please, I just want to talk," said the voice of a woman.

"Marjorie, it can't be, I killed you," he replied, confused.

"You thought you did, but I survived, Marcus. I'm here talking to you."

Victor leaned against the cage, the furrows of his brow questioning the possibility that Marjorie had somehow endured.

"Come outside and see for yourself."

Primrose recognised the voice immediately. What utter genius. Meg was messing with the mind of a psychopath, coaxing him to listen to the only person who had ever mattered to him. The person who had cared for him in the basement of the Pipers' house.

"I'm sorry, Marjorie, I had to kill you. You were talking to the police." Victor had taken the bait.

"It doesn't matter now, Marcus, I will look after you like I always did. Come to me, let me take you away from all this. Just you and me together again, remember?"

Victor had laid the knife aside, smitten by the voice of Marjorie. He was regressing into childhood memories, hugging his knees to his chest and rocking to the sound of Marjorie's calming voice.

Primrose eyed the knife, but it was out of her reach.

Tyla was regaining consciousness, the effects of the sedative waning rapidly. If she made a sudden move and distracted him she would surely die. Primrose tried to catch her attention, but Tyla was still groggy and unaware of the situation.

"Marjorie, I need you," he whispered.

"I'm coming. Stay right there, I'm coming to you."

Primrose prayed that Meg would move quickly. Tyla was moving around now and at any minute she could bring Victor to his senses.

The sound of glass smashing grabbed his attention. He climbed to his feet and headed towards the staircase.

"Marjorie," he called out. Only silence answered.

"I'm here, Marcus. I had to break the window to get in," Meg explained.

Tyla was fully awake now and rustling around on the plastic sheet. Victor glanced towards her, then back up the stairs.

Footsteps could be heard crossing the floor above and legs appeared at the top of the staircase.

Victor looked upwards. The woman was hidden in the shadow of the doorway.

"Marjorie?"

Meg didn't move. A sniper was aiming over her right shoulder, pointing his firearm directly at Victor.

"Come out with your hands up," he shouted, pushing Meg aside.

Victor was agile for his age. He raced across the floor towards Tyla, grabbing the knife as he reached her. He raised it high and then it fell and so did he.

The sound of a gunshot echoed loudly, hitting Victor in the shoulder of the arm that was holding the knife. The bullet pierced his skin, shattering the bone inside. He doubled as the pain exploded, dropping the knife beside Tyla, who grabbed it with her tiny fingers and plunged it into Victor's spine as he reeled beside her.

The basement was filling with police. Tyla was carried to safety and Primrose was attended by paramedics. Victor was carried to a waiting ambulance and driven to hospital with his wrists cuffed to the bed. Grayson followed behind; he wasn't going to let Victor, Felix, or Marcus out of his sight.

McGurn sighed with relief.

"Good work, Quinn, you just saved two lives," he praised.

Meg felt emotional. The realisation that she had finally saved someone was overwhelming. Fin was there to comfort her and she welcomed the warmth of his embrace.

McGurn headed for his car.

"Quinn," he shouted, "I think you should be the one to interview the bastard. See you tomorrow."

Meg accepted with a nod.

Tyla was fit to return home as Primrose headed for surgery to remove the damaged kidney.

Castleton turned towards his car as Meg wrapped her arms around Della and led her away. She turned to her husband. "Aren't you coming?" she questioned with a smile.

CHAPTER 45

The following morning Meg visited Florence Darby. She thought it only fair that the old woman should know the fate of her only child.

"How are you managing without Marjorie?" she enquired.

"Well Della seems to have taken her place, so all is well in my world, dear," replied the sweet old lady.

Meg knew that her friend had been checking on Florence since she learned the fate of her carer. It was good for Della and certainly good for Florence.

"You're becoming quite a regular visitor yourself." She smiled.

"I've come to deliver some news about your son," began Meg.

A tear formed in the corner of the old woman's eye. "Is it good news or bad?"

"Honestly, it's not terribly good news but I thought you would want to know."

Florence sipped at her tea quietly. Meg was uncertain how much information to reveal. She decided to leave it to Florence herself. If she asked a question Meg would answer honestly; if she didn't then she probably didn't want to know.

"Go ahead, tell me, I'm ready," declared Florence, setting her teacup on the table with a shaky hand.

"Last night we arrested a man for the murder of Marjorie. He is also responsible for the deaths of the Pipers, Sable Caine, Celia Tucker and five young children."

Meg paused as Florence digested the news.

"Oh my! How awful, but what has this got to do with Marcus?" She frowned.

"Marcus is the man we arrested."

Florence tossed her head backwards and fought to restrain the tears, but they flowed freely.

Meg touched her arm. "I'm so sorry, Florence, I wish I had something nicer to tell you."

"I'm grateful for your honesty, dear." She sniffed. "All these years I've wondered what became of him and now I know."

"He's currently in the hospital recovering from a bullet to the shoulder and a knife wound. I'm on my way there now to interview him, would you like to come with me?"

Florence pondered, wiping the tears from her cheeks. "I think after all this time I will have to decline, but thank you for the offer. I haven't set foot out of this house for decades. I don't think it is something I will ever do again, dear, unless it's in a wooden box. I would rather remember him as a small child, not a cold-blooded killer."

"I understand, Florence. If you change your mind I'm just at the end of the phone," soothed Meg.

Florence rose from the table and disappeared, returning with an album. She plucked a photograph of herself and Marcus from its pages and handed it to Meg.

"He won't remember me, but perhaps you would give him this, and tell him that I did love him even if it was only briefly."

Meg agreed and rose to leave.

"Tell me, Officer, is it my fault that he turned out this way?" queried Florence.

"Absolutely not," declared Meg. "Why would you even think that?"

"I was young, unmarried, unable to cope with a baby. Part of me was relieved when he went missing. Doesn't that make me a terrible mother?"

"Florence, that makes you human," consoled Meg. "The choices we make in life aren't always the right ones and we must live with the consequences, but trust me when I say, the path Marcus chose is a reflection of his failings, not yours."

***

Marcus Darby's hospital room was flanked by armed officers.

Meg stood at the window for a while, surveying the man responsible. He was an average-sized man with average features; there was nothing remarkable about him at all. He was the type of man you would pass daily on the street and never see. He was invisible to society, unnoticed and undetected. He was a neighbour, a colleague, a dog walker, he was all of these and more. He wore many faces, but the one he kept hidden was the most dangerous of them all.

Meg had read his file from the psychiatric unit. She knew the depravity of his own childhood but it did not justify his actions.

Fin arrived with coffees. "Thought you might need this."

"Thanks, I certainly do."

"Why are you standing on the corridor?"

"I'm psyching myself up to go in," she revealed.

"How did it go with Ms Darby?"

"She shed a tear, asked if it was because of her that he had turned out this way, and gave me this photograph to give him."

"She didn't want to visit him?"

"Would you in her position? I gave her the option and told her that if she changed her mind she should get in touch."

Castleton shrugged. "That's all you could do. Shall we go in?"

Marcus Darby was heavily bandaged around the shoulder and connected to a drip of clear fluid. Monitors around him flashed and beeped incessantly. A nurse was adjusting his pillows. One wrist was cuffed to the bed, while the other wandered freely.

"Aberbarry Police," stated Castleton. "Is he up to questioning?"

"I'd say so, but I'll inform the doctor that you're here, he may want to speak with you."

Marcus was cautioned, before Meg and Castleton took seats beside his bed.

"How are you feeling?" queried the DS.

"How do you think? I've a bullet hole in my shoulder and a knife wound in my back. Just missed my spinal cord, they said, child almost paralysed me," he grumbled.

"Ahh, but she didn't," snapped Meg sarcastically.

"Wasn't strong enough to drive it deep. I should have killed her before she had the chance."

Marcus displayed no remorse for his diabolical actions or empathy for the destruction of lives.

"I want to start by asking you about the Pipers. You lived with them for a while I believe?" began Meg.

"That's an understatement, lived with them. They treated their dog better than me," Marcus replied.

"And why was that?"

"They didn't want me. I lived in the basement like a feral animal, collared and caged for hours at a time. Some days they forgot to bring me water and food. I had no warmth, hardly any clothes, I ate bugs and drank my own pee," he snarled.

"But you didn't die, Marcus, you escaped."

"Yes, many years later after Marjorie came to live there. She fed me and I grew stronger. One day I saw my chance and took it."

"What happened then? Where did you go?"

"I lived on the streets, slept under bridges, on benches, doorways, anything was a step up from that house. Eventually I got a job as a labourer, bit of money in my pocket, and rented a place just outside London."

"How did you end up as a jeweller then?"

"I got taken on as an apprentice silversmith in Somerset, learned the trade. When I moved to Wales Mr Simeon was advertising for help. He offered me a job and when he died I inherited the shop."

Meg glanced at Castleton.

"You inherited the shop, how? Didn't Mr Simeon have any family?"

"He changed his will leaving it to me. The family weren't best pleased but it was what he wanted."

Castleton sensed deceit. Marcus had most probably threatened the old jeweller into changing his will. He made a note to investigate the cause of Mr Simeon's death. No doubt Marcus had something to do with that too.

"Okay, so when did the killings start?" demanded Meg.

Marcus went quiet. Was he avoiding the question or pondering the timeline?

"About thirty years ago, I'd say."

"Was it just children you targeted?"

"Yes, mostly, odd times someone would get in the way and I'd have to make an exception."

Marcus conversed freely as if this was the most normal of topics.

"We know about the five children you killed in this area, how many would you say there are in total?"

Meg already knew the answer, but she wanted to find out how truthful Marcus would be about his previous slayings. Behind the step of the basement staircase officers had discovered a biscuit tin containing forty-two locks of hair.

"It's hard to say without counting my..." He hesitated.

"Your trophies!"

"You found them?" he demanded, expressing surprise.

"Yes we found them. We will be able to identify every one of your victims from their hair samples."

Marcus frowned at the thought of his beloved treasure trove sitting in the hands of a stranger. "Can I have that back, when you've finished analysing?" he begged.

"Absolutely not," growled Meg.

"Forty-two children died by your hand, Mr Darby. Why?" fumed Castleton.

"You have a very low opinion of me, don't you, Officer?"

"It's nothing personal, I assure you, I'd have a very low opinion of anyone who murdered so many innocent children."

"I was once an innocent child too," barked Marcus. "No one gives a thought to that, do they?"

Meg took the lead.

"Plenty of people have difficult childhoods, Marcus, it doesn't turn them all into serial killers."

"I was never treated like a child, never had a childhood in the sense of the word. Imagine never seeing daylight until you reach fifteen. All those years locked in a basement, in a cage, never hearing a kind word or feeling a warm hug."

Meg felt a twinge of sympathy develop as Marcus described his young life.

"Killing the Pipers I understand, revenge for the way they treated you, but young children, that's the bit that puzzles me."

"When I moved to Pollard Avenue, I was surprised to learn that the Pipers were still living there. Mr Piper continued to be involved with paedophilia and Mrs Piper was turning a blind eye like usual. They had no idea who I was when they invited me into their home. I took great delight in slaughtering them, but not before I revealed my identity. The world is a much better place without them."

"That's what people will think of you, Marcus," stated Meg.

"Absolutely not. When the world knows my story there will be an outpouring of sympathy. I will be a national hero, ridding society of perverse individuals preying on the weak and innocent."

Meg shared a look with Castleton and shrugged her shoulders. Marcus could not identify with his own wrongdoings, choosing to focus on the failures of others instead.

"I'm afraid you'll be going to prison for a very long time, Mr Darby," scoffed Meg. "You'll never be free again."

Marcus looked dejected as the thought had honestly never crossed his mind.

"I wanted them to feel like I did," he announced, "captive, caged, degraded, crying for my mother."

"But they were innocent, just like you were when the Pipers abducted you. Their failings as human beings were not your fault, nor was it the fault of the children you slaughtered. You killed them, Marcus, in the most heinous of ways. That's not what happened to you."

"What else could I do, set them free and wait for the police to arrive? That was the only way to secure my anonymity," he pleaded.

"You could have stopped, Marcus, at any time," added Castleton, "but you liked it too much, didn't you?"

Meg and Castleton exchanged a look of disgust.

"Let's move on to Sable Caine."

"She was taking pictures of me, I saw the flash of her camera one night, she had to die. I couldn't let images circulate. I worked so hard on being inconspicuous."

"What about Celia Tucker? The poor woman was paralysed, what had she ever done to you?"

"She knew too much, sitting by the window day after day, watching, keeping note of my movements. Marjorie said she was using an alphabet board. I knew it wouldn't be long before she gave me up."

Meg thought back to the last session she had held with Celia, when the poor woman was insistent that the blind man was the murderer. Celia died because she could not communicate, or rather that no one took enough time to listen. Marjorie was hiding the alphabet board. Did she know that the blind man and Marcus Darby were one and the same? Meg felt the pang of guilt prod at her conscience. Poor Celia, had the woman not already suffered enough?

"I should have been more patient with Celia," she scolded herself.

Castleton touched her arm. "No one could have known Celia's fate. Don't blame yourself, blame him." He tossed a look towards the murderer laid uncaring before them. "He won't lose sleep over any of this."

Castleton was right.

"Let's move on then," sighed Meg. "Finally we have Marjorie Kimble, your last victim and supposedly your friend."

"I hadn't realised that she was my Marjorie. She cared for me, but said nothing. I'm not even sure that she knew who I was."

"She may not have worked out who you were but she certainly knew you were back in the area. She was protecting you without realising it. She didn't know that the blind man she cared for was the boy she had helped years earlier. Until maybe that night when you visited her apartment and killed her."

"She was an unfortunate consequence," sighed Marcus nonchalantly.

"Is that how you see her? The girl who helped you through childhood, the only friend you had in the world was nothing more than an unfortunate consequence?" gasped Meg.

Marcus nodded.

"You see the world in a very different way to the rest of us Mr Darby," added Castleton.

"And who's to say that your way is right?"

"Oh I know it is, Marcus, of that I'm certain."

"There's nothing certain in life, Detective," he gloated.

"Can I ask about your time in the psychiatric unit and the 'brothers' that you fabricated? You did fabricate them, didn't you?" quizzed Meg.

Marcus grinned maliciously. "Now that would be telling, Officer."

"I think you constructed the personas to avoid a jail sentence."

"Victor and Felix were my friends. I fashioned them to fight the loneliness and the dark of the basement. For a long time they became real to me, an extension of my own personality. I talked to them and they talked back. When I was arrested it was easy to introduce them to the psychiatrist and convince him that my psyche was fractured. I fabricated the others to add weight to my performance."

Castleton rose and strolled to the window, taking in a breath of fresh air. It was hard to remain impartial in the presence of such malevolence.

"I think we're done here," exclaimed Meg.

"What happens now?" Marcus queried.

"When you're fit for discharge you'll be taken to the police station where you'll be formally charged and then held on remand until your court hearing."

"Can I ask how you discovered it was me? I was always so very careful."

"It was the watch."

Marcus touched his wrist, feeling for the watch that usually sat there. "Where is it?" he pleaded, as if the watch were of strong significance to him.

"It's in an evidence bag back at the station," informed Castleton.

"It had sentimental value?" enquired Meg.

"It belonged to Edward Piper. The night I killed him I stole it from his wrist. It was the symbol of my eternal freedom and his demise. It was his most prized possession handed down through generations of his family. It was extremely rare and very valuable."

"It was also your downfall," sneered Castleton.

"What became of the Pipers' car?" questioned Meg.

"You'll find it swimming with the fishes at the bottom of the lake," he scoffed.

Meg withdrew the photograph from her pocket and placed beside Marcus. "Your mother sent this. She wanted you to have it and to know that she loved you."

Marcus grasped the photograph and held it to his chest. "Is she still alive?" he demanded.

"Yes."

"Can I see her?"

"I'm afraid she doesn't want to see you."

Marcus stared in disbelief. "She doesn't want to see her own child? What kind of mother is she?" he growled.

"The very best kind," replied Meg.

"Then why won't she see me?"

"Because you're no longer her child, Marcus, you're nothing but a monster!" snarled Castleton leaving the room.

In the hallway, a white coat approached.

"When will he be fit for discharge?" asked Castleton.

"Pretty soon, his vitals are stable. The knife wound was superficial and the bullet has been removed. His shoulder has been pinned together, but that won't delay his discharge," informed the doctor.

"Let's grab a bite to eat, shall we? The canteen is downstairs," suggested Castleton, desperately in need of sustenance. "Can you believe that guy?"

"These days I can believe anything," replied Meg.

"Well one good thing has come out of all this misery, I suppose." He grinned.

"What's that?"

"The two of us getting back together."

"Is that what we're doing?" teased Meg.

As they sat down to eat a bleep flashed in the pocket of the white coat sitting at the next table. "Cardiac arrest, room 28," he informed his colleague as they rushed from the cafeteria, abandoning half-eaten chicken dinners.

"Room 28!" exclaimed Meg. "Isn't that Marcus Darby's room?"

Castleton nodded. They grabbed their lunch and hurried in the direction of the murderer's room.

Outside, Ewan Davis was standing alone. "I'm the relief while they get some lunch," he explained.

"What's going on in there?" asked Meg.

"Machines were going crazy then a flock of white coats appeared. Looks like they're giving CPR. Cardiac arrest, I guess."

Meg waited for the commotion to settle then heard a male voice say, "I'm calling it, the time's 12.50, all in agreement?"

The posse of medics exited the room, one doctor from earlier stopping to explain, "We did everything we could, but I'm afraid we lost him."

"He's dead?" confirmed Meg.

"I'm afraid so."

"Couldn't have happened to a more deserving person," muttered Davis. "I hope he goes straight to hell."

Meg entered the room, where the body of Marcus Darby was covered by a white sheet. The photograph he had clutched lay crumpled on the floor beside him.

She crossed to the window and looked out. At first her thoughts were directed to Constable Davis, whose sudden appearance outside the murderer's room seemed coincidental. Davis had erred his feelings quite ferociously. Marcus Darby's death would not keep him awake at night, but Meg did not think Davis capable of eliminating the murderer, even though he had motive in the form of his partner Primrose Swann, who was lying only a corridor away.

Then she saw her crossing the car park and unlocking the jalopy of a vehicle she called a car. Della Warren was driving away.

CHAPTER 46

The next evening when Tyla and Joel had said goodnight, Meg and Della sat alone for their final night together. Meg and Fin were returning to Brightmarsh the following day. He'd gone to meet up with his colleagues for a farewell drink and Meg had opted to spend her time with Della.

Meg opened a bottle of Prosecco. "Thought we'd push the boat out," she giggled.

"God, I'm going to miss you," stated Della, chinking her glass against Meg's.

"Really? Thought you'd be glad to see the back of me. It's been quite a ride!"

"It certainly has, and I really do appreciate you giving up for your life for the last couple of months to spend it with me."

"There wasn't much of a life to give up, Della, not back then."

"You've sorted things out now though?"

"Yeah, I think we have. Hopefully, anyway. I guess we won't know for certain until we're back home."

"You certainly seem a lot happier than when you arrived."

"Yes, I am. I think I finally conquered my demons. I saved Tyla and Primrose. I'm feeling pretty positive about life now."

"How is Primrose?"

"She's okay, returning to work in a week or so. Davis has been clucking over her like a mother hen. He cares for her in a 'partner' kind of way."

"It's nice to have someone who cares."

"Speaking of which, who are the flowers from? Is there something I should know?"

Della blushed slightly, admiring the bouquet of roses sitting on the table. "They're from Patrick," she declared coyly.

"Oh, Patrick," mused Meg, rolling her eyes at Della. "That was thoughtful of him."

"He seems a nice guy."

"He is, Della, I really hope you two get it together."

"There was a connection every time I saw him, but we'll see. The flowers are a nice touch though."

They drank and chatted the hours away, until Fin returned a little worse for wear.

"I think I better get this one to bed," said Meg, holding the inebriated Fin up against the wall.

"I think you might need a hand getting him upstairs."

Fin glanced from Meg to Della and smirked. "I'm not sure I can handle both of you tonight," he chuckled.

"Don't worry," replied Meg, "you're not going to be that lucky."

Fin collapsed on the bed as Della headed for the door.

She paused for a moment, looking back at Meg, who was struggling to undress her husband.

"Meg, there's something I need to tell you," she proffered solemnly.

Meg glanced towards her. "No need, Della, I already know."

A silent moment passed between them, the two women conscious of its significance.

Marcus Darby had died of a haemorrhage, the pathologist declared. No inquest was needed.

Meg and Della knew the truth, and that was exactly how it would remain.

***

On the journey home, they dropped in at the station to celebrate McGurn's retirement. In the aftermath of the last few months he'd decided to call time on his illustrious career, choosing to leave on a triumphant note.

"Thanks for your help. I couldn't have done it without you," praised McGurn.

"One question, sir?" begged Meg, choosing not to revel in the DCI's praise. "What will happen to Marcus Darby's watch."

McGurn thought for a moment. "I suppose it will sit in storage, why do you ask?"

"I wondered, since there's no family to pass it on to, could his mother have it?"

"Do you think she would want it?"

"I think it would help to pay for full-time carers for her. She's suffering dementia and I know that Della helps out, but she really could use the support. That way something useful would come out of it, a kind gesture for a very kind old lady."

"Leave it with me. I'll see what I can do."

Meg passed between the colleagues she had now come to call friends, stopping at Patrick Grayson.

"Do me a favour, Inspector?" she asked.

Grayson nodded.

"Look after Della for me."

Grayson smiled and nodded.

Primrose had made the party too, with the aid of Ewan, insistent on pushing her in a wheelchair.

"Looking good, Swann," declared Meg.

"Feeling it now too. Thanks, Meg, you saved my life. I owe you one."

"You don't owe me a thing, Constable, I'm just glad things turned out the way they did."

"Have you heard?" interrupted Briggs. "They've managed to get DNA from all the samples of hair."

"That's brilliant news," cheered Meg.

The team raised a glass to McGurn and the eventual success of a difficult and traumatic case, stopping to spare a tender thought for those who had lost their lives in the process.

***

Leaving Aberbarry was emotional. It had been a rollercoaster ride of tragedy and uncertainty, but at least Meg and Fin were leaving it together.

"Don't you think it was weird how Marcus Darby suddenly died?" queried Castleton moments into their journey.

"I suppose so, but think of it as karma," replied Meg. "No one deserved it more than he."

"I'd rather hoped he would end his days like he began them, in a cage," added Fin.

"Me too, but the world is full of inexplicable mystery, best not to dissect it," replied Meg. "Besides, it's over now."

"You don't think Davis had anything to do with it, do you? It seems odd how he suddenly appeared and moments later Darby was dead."

Meg wanted desperately to avoid a conversation about the murderer's demise. She turned on the radio, hoping that Fin would be distracted by music.

"I think you should stop with the questions now, Sergeant. The case is solved and the culprit is dead," she advised. "I think we should talk about something else instead."

"Like what?" Fin quizzed.
"Well, did you know that trees cry?" she began.

ABOUT THE AUTHOR

Writing has been a passion of mine since early childhood, but time has always been a factor that I could not afford, as my family took priority.

Now, at almost sixty, my publishing dream has become a reality with my first novel, *When The Raven Sings* coming to fruition in June 2023.

I hope to continue writing for my pleasure and hopefully the pleasure of those who read my books.

- amazon.com/stores/A-G-Nuttall/author/B0C7N75J7K
- bookbub.com/authors/a-g-nuttall
- goodreads.com/agnuttall

Printed in Great Britain
by Amazon